MEDITATION CAN BE MURDER

THE WITCH OF HENBANE ISLAND
BOOK 1

POPPY BRIDGEMAN

Ebook ISBN: 978-1-990509-35-3
Paperback ISBN: 978-1-990509–36-0
Audio book ISBN:978-1-990509-37-7

Cover created by Getcovers

FREE EBOOK

Claim your copy of Magic Will Out when you use the QR code to sign up for my newsletter and follow Cossi's search for her identity as a witch.

1

Mr. Crablee's office was too warm. I was here because my dad died a week ago and now apparently, he'd left me something in his will. The lawyer's office was warm, like I said, and stuffy, and dimly lit. I sat in a hard chair facing his worn brown leather one over the top of his boring oak desk. I'd been here fifteen minutes, and no one had checked on me or given me an update on his timing.

Or offered water, coffee, or tea. It was like I'd slipped into an alternate universe run on blah.

The door opened behind me. I turned to see a man enter. No one I knew, he was as medium as it got. Grey hair, grey eyes, grey suit, I'd swear his skin was some kind of beige grey.

"Ms. Fortuna?" he asked like he expected someone else to be sitting here.

"Yes."

"Cosmos Fortuna?"

"Do you need to see ID?" I wasn't usually rude like this,

at least I don't think of myself that way. Waiting had worn out my last nerve. Dad was dead, I was an orphan at twenty-one, I had no idea what I was going to do with my life, and I had no one to bitch to about it.

"Yes, please. I want to be certain I'm dealing with the right person. You understand."

I pulled out my driver's license and handed it over. Whatever dad left me couldn't be worth all this. We had nothing beyond the money to pay our bills.

"Thank you." He took my ID and sat in the chair across from mine. He placed a file on the desk. It was gray, I hadn't even noticed it in his hand, then picked up a pen and wrote my details on a legal pad. He added something I couldn't read, then put the date on top and a line for me to sign.

"I have the letter here," he said, tapping the file folder. "You sign for receipt, and I will deliver it to you as directed by your father."

Probably an overdue bill, I thought as I scribbled my name on the line.

Mr. Crablee handed me an envelope, one of those business-sized ones. "You can read it here. I'll give you some privacy. If you need anything or have any questions, please ask the receptionist to find me."

Then I was alone. Like my whole life ahead of me was. Cossi Fortuna, lonely and pathetic orphan.

I picked up a letter opener from Crablee's desk and slit the top of the envelope. Normally I would just rip it open, but it was from Dad. I wanted to keep it nice.

His handwriting filled a single sheet of unlined paper.

Cossi, I'm sorry I am not there for you. I love you and I've done my best to protect you, but now you must have the truth.

The truth? Was I an heiress? Maybe Mom and Dad hid here in Vancouver to protect me. And I guess it was also possible he'd kidnapped me as a kid. I really didn't want to read on, but I couldn't seem to stop.

We lived on an island just off the Sunshine coast. It's a special place, and we would have stayed forever, but one day your mother made a mistake. It was a doozie. We had to leave, so we packed up fast and brought you here. And we lied from the first day we arrived until now.

The kidnapping was suddenly feeling a bit less far-fetched.

There's no way to build up to this or soften what is probably going to be a shock. You are a witch. Your mother was a witch. I was a witch.

There, it's out. And I feel a lot lighter. Of course, I won't be there to help you get through the next few days. Now that you've been told, your powers will be freed. You need to find a community to train you.

I fought against the pull to keep reading. This couldn't be true. What powers? What island? There were communities for people with real magic? I kicked my toe against the desk leg. Yup, it hurt. I wasn't dreaming.

I can't be sure what your powers are, but you will have three. They may connect, or they may be very different. You'll find what you need to locate a community in my journal. It's hidden in the house. In my bedroom, inside the heating grate. I wrote it on the most recent page only a few days ago.

Find your people but stay away from our old home. I can't name the island. We are all under a compulsion spell to keep it secret, but please remember that we couldn't go back. It will not be a healthy place for you.

Your mother and I love you, no matter that we are dead. I am sorry for leaving you alone here.

I refolded the letter and slipped it into the envelope. Mr. Crablee would have no answers for me, and maybe he'd call someone who would lock me up in some kind of facility for believing what Dad wrote. But I did. I have no idea why, but there was no doubt in my mind that I was a witch, and somewhere out there was a whole community for me, and I wouldn't be alone anymore.

2

————

Home. It wasn't much, just a two-bedroom in an old house that had been subdivided into an apartment on each floor. We had the basement, and it always seemed cozy to me, but now it just felt dark and unwelcoming.

I turned on the tap to get water for tea and looked out at the small slice of garden we'd been allotted. There wasn't much to see because only about half of the basement was above ground. But Dad planted our patch with all kinds of weird flowers and herbs. I'd never understood why, but now I guess he made potions or something. Thinking about it gave me a headache. Too many things rolling around in my brain.

When the tea was ready, I went into Dad's bedroom with a screwdriver. The heating grate was on the bottom of the wall facing his bed. I worked the screws, and there was his journal taped to the duct just inside. At least he wasn't lying about that like he'd done about everything else in my life.

I curled up in his chair and, despite my current anger, I

felt safe. I mean, he shouldn't have kept such a big secret, but he was a great dad in other ways. I would miss him forever.

He'd started the journal just before we got to Vancouver. The spell I needed was on the last page, but I turned to the first one. If I was going to follow his wishes, I wanted to know more about my past.

Mom did screw up. One of the first entries described her mistake, and I didn't think Dad expected me to look this far back because there was the name of the place we left. Henbane Island. It was under a compulsion to keep the people living on the mainland from finding it. Only witches, or I guess whatever other magic people lived there, could find it.

Until for a second my mom exposed it. I didn't understand what she actually did, or why, but I guess I could see why they decided to leave.

The next entries were all about getting away. A boat to the mainland, a ferry to Vancouver, and finding this place in Kitsilano. I turned on the light because it got dark early in the basement no matter the season.

The next few pages were boring, setting up home, finding jobs, blah blah blah. I started flipping pages, looking for more interesting stuff, but it seemed like my parents wanted to hide anything different about us. Then I got to the date my mother died, my eleventh birthday.

One day Cossi will be alone, Dad had written. Yeah, well, that day was about a week ago. I graduated from business school with all kinds of plans to be my own boss, then Dad died. And now this bombshell. I flipped to the last entry.

I've given our lawyer a letter explaining everything, and you are reading this journal, Cossi, so I'm gone.

I won't repeat the letter, but here's what you do to find a community. You won't know it, but your magic will power the spell. Gather rosemary and thyme from the garden. Take a handful of twigs from the licorice jar, and then light the fire. Toss the herbs on when it's in full flame and say who you are, your phone number and what you want, a home. Someone will answer you within a few minutes. They will tell you where to go.

That was easy. No incantations or eye of newt. Our fireplace was clean, with logs and kindling ready to go. Had Dad done that in his last few hours? No point in waiting. I gathered what I needed, lit the fire and waited for it to get a steady burn.

The doorbell rang before the flames were high enough.

Doreen Miller, our landlady. I guess she was mine now. "Hi, what can I do for you?" I kept my voice sweet; I'd need to be on her good side for a while until I could move or find a way to pay the rent. Who knows how long it would be before I could get to a witchy community?

"I'm sorry, Cosmos." She held out an envelope.

I opened it to find an eviction notice with a date in two days. WHAT?

"You can't just kick me out like that." My hand was shaking. I was about to be homeless, and I was an orphan, and there were no orphanages for people my age.

"This is the final notice. Your father ignored the previous ones. Please know I tried. He left me with no choice."

One more lie from dad. Or maybe not. I had no way to prove she'd done the right thing. And frankly, I didn't have the energy to pursue it.

I shut the door in her face. I was still the legal tenant, and there was no reason for me to be polite.

Back in the living room, I tossed the eviction notice in the fire and waited for it to turn to ashes before I tossed in the rosemary, thyme, and licorice.

Nothing happened. Then I remembered I had to tell the fire some things.

"I'm Cosmos Fortuna. I need a home." I rattled off my phone number and then went back to sit in Dad's chair and wait.

3

————

I'd barely touched the seat of the chair when my phone rang. It couldn't be that fast. It was probably some debt collector. I mean, I had no confidence that I wouldn't be hounded out of the house by all kinds of unsavory, and savory, characters. My anger was twisting up my grief again.

"Yes?" I said.

"Cosmos Fortuna?" It was a man's voice. Older, close to Dad's age.

"That's me." I kept my voice neutral. It could still be a debt collector.

"I heard your call," he said. "My name is Phillip Raziel."

Not a name I knew, but that wasn't a surprise. He was some kind of witch, and as far as I knew, I had never met one. Well, my parents, but that doesn't count. Although, if they kept their identities so well hidden, maybe everyone was a witch.

"Thank you for calling," I said and immediately felt like an idiot, but what do you say when someone answers a spell?

"You are looking for a home and you seem to be in a hurry," he said.

So my panic got through in the smoke? "It's all happened really fast, and I have to leave my home in the next couple of days. Can you help me?"

"That's why I called. We are inviting you to join us. I suppose we may be the first, but I knew your parents. If that helps at all."

Was I shopping for a home that was right for me? Or desperate to take whatever was offered? "You are the first to call," I said. "Where is your community?"

"Your father didn't tell you?"

"He didn't tell me anything until after he died." Why did I say that? Was it because this Phillip guy seemed to be a sympathetic ear, or was he casting a spell on me?

"You are able to speak to the dead?"

I would not enjoy that. Images of moldy, smelly ghosts yelling at me all the time held no appeal at all. "No. He left a letter. Look, I don't have a car, or much of a travel budget, so I'm kind of limited to where I can go. Where is your community?"

"An island off Sechelt."

So, the exact place Dad told me to avoid.

"I don't know how to get there," I said. I was stalling because I didn't know how to tell him I couldn't accept, and I was terrified that no one else would call.

"Ferry from Horseshoe Bay to Langdale. If you tell us which sailing, we'll arrange for a taxi to pick you up and bring you to our meeting point. Does this mean you will join us?"

I got another call. Maybe the whole issue of defying Dad for the first time would be put on hold.

"I have another call, Mr. Raziel. Can I reach out later?"

"Certainly. Just reach out on this number."

I don't think he liked being put off, but he kept it polite.

I ended up with three offers in ten minutes. This witch thing was good for my ego. Now I had to decide. The first thing was to think through the idea of moving to a magical community. I was so tied up with picking from the responses to my spell that I hadn't even considered just finding a job and apartment and staying in Vancouver. I mean, I didn't have a support group here, no friends, no relatives, nothing. Was that why I jumped at the chance to make a giant change rather than a tiny one?

The island, Henbane, was my first choice. Not because Dad said not to go, I'm not fifteen and in full rebellion mode. Because they called first. And this Phillip guy knew my dad. And I really wanted to know where I came from. And meet people who could talk about my family.

I didn't have much to pack, all the furniture came with the place. There wasn't much food in the cupboards. My clothes and the herbs Dad had put up would fit in a backpack, the one I used when I was studying. I had no one to say goodbye to.

I looked up the ferry schedule. There were still two sailings. I might just make the first one, before I could triple guess my decision. I called Mr. Raziel and said I would come. That I'd text from the ferry to confirm my arrival. He replied with a happy face and a thumbs up emoji.

Ten minutes later I'd changed into more comfortable clothes, packed everything I owned and was ready to catch the first of two buses. One last look into the garden to say goodbye and I'd be gone.

A shape moved between the raised beds. In the dusk it

seemed to slink. Then it stepped into a lighter patch. It was the upstairs neighbor's cat. Another thought popped into my head; maybe I could have a cat as my familiar. Would I get a broom to ride?

You'll be lucky. Where had that thought come from?

4

The taxi picked me up at the ferry terminal. I wondered if the driver was a magic person. I really needed to find another way to phrase it, like, were they all witches? Were there more kinds? Was it polite to ask?

I arrived at the house just around midnight because of course I missed the first ferry. The key was exactly where Mr. Raziel said it would be, inside the letter slot in the door, on a string. I tossed my backpack on the floor, ready to grab it on my way out as soon as my escort arrived. Then I saw the envelope on the narrow table in the hall. My full name printed out in some violet ink. *Cosmos Fortuna.*

Inside was a short note.

Make yourself at home. We will collect you in the morning, probably by seven am. It is far too dangerous to navigate to the island in the dark. It was signed P with all the flourishes of a calligrapher's dream.

So here I was in a strange house, in a strange town, waiting to be taken to a strange island. I was filled to the brim with questions that would have to wait until tomorrow.

I fairly vibrated with expectations that were not going to be met.

Sleep wasn't going to be an option until I settled, so I took a tour of the house. I'd never been inside a Victorian before. It was all we could do to afford the basement suite, and my education was only possible because I won a bunch of scholarships and lived at home.

The downstairs contained a parlor, a tiny powder room, and a kitchen. In there was a door which I assumed was the basement, but it was locked solid. With spells?

Upstairs, two more bedrooms, a dressing room and a big bathroom completed my tour. I still buzzed with unresolved excitement, and there was no point in unpacking anything to lay on a bed with my eyes wide open.

I returned to the kitchen and found some hot chocolate mix in a cupboard. The fridge had fresh milk, butter, and a loaf of bread. I made the cocoa in a pan on the range because there was no microwave. I wondered if someone lived here normally. Or was the fridge stocked for me? I wasn't sure I liked the idea of camping in someone's house when they were away, but Mr. Raziel told me to come.

The parlor had bookshelves stocked with enough reading material for a lifetime. I grabbed a copy of an old spy thriller, curled up on the sofa and wrapped the knitted throw around me for warmth.

My eyes drooped and then popped open. Stupid brain. Now I was committed, my mind came up with a question I couldn't answer. I could fret over it all night though. What if this was an elaborate plot to get me on the island to punish me for my mother's mistake?

.   .   .

I WAS WOKEN up by the sound of a door opening. The room was flooded with light from the windows. I jerked up and tried to make myself presentable, but no way would my hair cooperate by forming into something less like an abandoned bird's nest. It barely cooperated when I took an hour to force it.

A middle-aged man walked in. Tall, wiry, nicely trimmed beard, and bright green eyes. Not what I expected from a male witch. He smiled at me and took off his coat.

"I see you got some rest," he said.

I blushed like I was caught doing something wrong. "Are we leaving now?"

"I like your eagerness. I'm not sure how I would react to such a revelation."

Probably take it in stride, I thought. This guy oozed confidence. "I don't know if I've had time to react," I said. "It's only been a day."

"Let's get you some breakfast and then we'll head to the boat."

5

Despite my eagerness to get going, Mr. Raziel sent me up to the bathroom to brush my teeth and change into something warmer while he made toast and tea.

"Before we go," he said when I was sitting at the table, "there are some rules on the island. And you probably have some questions."

I was all questions, but as soon as he asked, they all disappeared from my brain. I mean, this was a whole new reality. "Maybe you should start, Mr. Raziel," I said. I might come up with some reasonable questions if I knew a little about where I was headed.

"Call me Phillip," he said. "It's not complicated. The first and most crucial rule is no one can learn about the island. It's not safe for our kind if the normal world finds out about us."

"You mean like witch trials?"

"No. We worry about being exploited these days. What do you think the criminal world would do to get a magic user on their team?"

"Would someone do that? I mean, a magical person, or whatever you—I mean, we, call ourselves."

"Witches, shifters, whatever we are. There isn't really a collective for the whole world of magic."

"Okay, I'll have no problem keeping the island a secret. What other rules?"

"We all contribute," Phillip said. "Either you work, or you run a business. We keep to all the same kind of red tape as normal people. We pay our taxes; we register our businesses. Our doctors have licenses, our police have training, and our teachers are certified. Most of what we need is available on the island."

"But if it's a secret... how do you get mail, or deliveries, or anything not magical?" Should I turn back and look for a community on the mainland? Someplace that doesn't require so much work.

"This house is the address for the entire island. It's worked for more than a hundred years, Cosmos."

"Call me Cossi," I said. I hated my full name because people assumed it was that Greek name. I was named after a flower that symbolized harmony and balance, both of which were in short supply right now. "So is there a job waiting for me? Where will I live?"

"Your situation is a bit unusual. The council agreed you needed a few months to settle in. So you have time to find a job. If you're okay with it, you can stay with me. I have spare rooms."

That seemed wrong, moving in with this older guy. "How will I pay my way while I'm looking for a job?"

"If you don't have any money, we will pay your bills. If you prefer, it can be a loan. We want you to succeed, Cossi. I must tell you I'm glad you didn't hold your family's history against us. I've hoped for your return for a long time."

I'd done everything I could to avoid debt, but I wasn't a charity case. "A loan would be great. And I don't want to come across wrong, but what other accommodation is available?"

"There are no hotels," Phillip said. "Other residents may have rooms to rent, they do that when we have other witches visit. Perhaps you can wait to make that decision until we arrive?"

"Anything else?" I wanted to go to the island with some facts. Not that I was going to run away, but I needed a bit of firm ground.

"We're a peaceful community. We do have disagreements, but nothing larger." He took our plates and put them in the sink. "We have a shifter community on one end of the island. But mostly we're witches."

"So what happens if someone gets sick? Or hurt?"

"Anything serious we bring to the mainland. We're not hiding from the world because we don't want what it has to offer, Cossi. We have computers, bank accounts, and smartphones. We're hiding because it's too risky not to protect ourselves."

"One more," I said. This question couldn't wait until I was on an island and dependent on someone to get back. My stomach filled with acid as I contemplated the worst-case answer. "What about my mother's history on the island?"

He nodded and thought for a second. Was that because he was making up a story? I didn't get a lying vibe off him, but he was definitely uncomfortable.

"What your mother did was a mistake, Cossi." He didn't turn to face me as he spoke. "We are people as well as witches. Most of the island's inhabitants know she didn't do it on purpose, and wish she'd stayed to face the consequences. Some will look at you and see her. I'm sure you can handle a little opposition."

Why did I get the feeling he was one of the people who was glad she'd left?

"Okay. I guess I can wait until we get there before I come up with more questions." And I'd make sure I asked a lot of them.

"Then help me with the dishes, and we'll go."

I could see why no one wanted to do this trip at night. We got on the boat, too small in my opinion, but I'd never been a water baby. We headed out to the open ocean. Then, just when I was about to mention my fear of drowning, Phillip said something I didn't understand, and land appeared. We'd gone around the back of the island, somehow not crashing into rocks or a sandbar.

The dock was just the end of a street where boats were tied up on a small wooden side dock. There were a couple of other vessels moored here, but half a block away I could see a store on each side of the street. No cars.

"We'll go to my place so you can decide if you want to stay and drop off your pack. No time better than now to take you around the island for orientation."

How was I going to decide where I'd stay if he didn't show me alternatives? I just nodded and decided to go along with it. I could always move out tomorrow, right?

Phillip tied up the boat and helped me onto the dock. "I own the bookstore," he said. "I'll introduce you to a few people before we go on our tour."

. . .

THE FIRST THREE stores we passed were vacant, but someone was taking care of them because there was no dust or debris outside, or boards on the windows. They looked like the new tenant was about to move in. My business school brain started thinking about stocking the shelves with product. Just what product I had no idea.

"The park is where we hold community meetings if the weather is favorable." Phillip didn't slow down so I could only concentrate on the stores we walked past. The other side of the street had businesses, but getting their names would be for another day unless I was willing to lose my guide.

We passed a hardware store called Make it Right that had a sign about technology services and products in the window, a cozy looking cafe, A Bite and a Sip, and a tea and potions store called Sweet and Bitter. Phillip stopped at the bookstore, Raziel's Reads, and held the door for me. "I live above the store; we all do on Main Street, so we don't have far to go for work."

The entrance to his apartment was through an archway in the back behind books on Druidic rituals.

"Is this the only way in?" I asked. It seemed a bit inconvenient to have to go through the store if I was out late.

"There's a side door," Phillip said. "If you stay, I'll give you the key. I'm sure you don't want me knowing when you come and go after you've settled."

His living quarters were bigger than our old basement suite. Two bedrooms with a bathroom each, a cozy library, a living room with a giant TV, and a decently sized kitchen.

"Drop your backpack in the far bedroom," Phillip said. "The outside door is just across the hall."

I did as he said because I was way more interested in seeing more of my new home than just his place. "How do we get around?" I asked. "I didn't see any cars."

"None on the island. It's just easier to use a bike or a horse." He handed me a key and we went through the private exit to the side of the building.

"Do you ride?" he asked. "I can ask to borrow a horse and a buggy, but it's slow."

"I know how to ride a bike," I assured him. "I guess I'll need to buy one."

"You can, but there are enough community bikes to borrow. You can keep one close for a few days, or simply drop it off every time you've finished with it."

On the opposite side of the street was a pet store, Run, Fly, Slither. I'd head in there as soon as Phillip was done with the tour. Maybe I could adopt a familiar right away. Phillip led me to the cafe and introduced me to the owner, a cute hipster named Jan.

"We're heading out for the tour," Phillip said. "I thought Cossi and I could come by afterwards for lunch."

Jan smiled and it lit up his face. "I'll put on something special to welcome you."

"We can take the tour of the island now," Phillip said. "Or I can introduce you to the other merchants first?"

It was an easy decision. I wanted to see my home for the first time. I knew everything would be there if we waited, but I couldn't help thinking that if we delayed then he would find a reason to keep putting it off. I knew right then everything made me wonder if I was feeling my magic, but some of it must be, right? And I didn't care. Something was pushing me to tour the island.

"Let's get the bikes and ride before the day is too far gone," I said enthusiastically.

"We won't do the whole island," he said. "To the west is Shifter territory, the east is the earth witch compound. We'll leave those for now. Today is more of a survey."

Shifters? What the heck, was there some kind of full moon rule? I didn't want to ask and look like an idiot, or a bigot, or... I don't know, someone who'd woken up as a witch only a day ago.

I'd let him decide on the route. I had the rest of my life to explore, and if I made a friend, it would be more fun to explore with someone younger.

The bike park was easy to negotiate. Phillip told me that people who owned bikes didn't use it, so any ride there was up for grabs. I noticed a few trailers in the corner, some like the ones people put their kids in, and two that were much larger. Apparently, these were used for deliveries and hauling drunks home from the bar next to the shifter village.

It only took just over an hour to do our little tour. The paths were well maintained, and really it was a small island. I saw the residential area, or at least part of it, there was a small clinic about five minutes east of Main and a school at the other end of the island. Apparently, all the usual subjects were taught, and spell casting, which explained the need for distance.

On a cliff overlooking the west shore, there was a set of five shelters. They were built in the shape of tepees, but more permanent.

I asked Phillip what they were.

"Occasionally some of the residents need solitude to devise more complicated spells or simply reflect and restore. They come here for a few days."

The place looked deserted, like no one had needed solitude for decades. "Does anyone own them?" I asked.

Now I was at least oriented, I'd started to think what I could do to make a living. I vowed, only to myself, that I'd support myself as fast as possible. Get my own home, get a job or a business going. Anything to avoid being a burden.

"I suppose they are owned by the community," he said. "Why?"

"It looks like they need some maintenance," I said.

He looked at his watch and then at the tents. "We should get back. I'm sure Jan has invited a few people to our lunch. Everyone will want to meet you."

L unch was amazing. I would need to check out the other cafe, but this was going to be my favorite, well, as soon as I could afford to eat out.

Phillip had been right about other people. Jan invited the woman who owned the pet store, or maybe it was a familiar store. Lilibeth Archer was about my age and dark skinned, with freckles across her nose. Lance Volk, a shifter. He helped run the bar on the edge of shifter territory. Red hair and tanned skin that went well with his intense, greenish gray eyes. And one more guy. D Rothtect, a good-looking nerd who ran the tech support for the island residents.

"I'll leave you to get acquainted," Phillip said.

Jan placed my rice bowl on the table and joined us. "I didn't want to bring too many people in," he said. "I figured you could wait to meet the older witches."

"Thanks. I don't know anyone here, or about being a witch, or anything about this world," I said.

"Don't worry," Lilibeth said. "We'll help you get settled. It's not that complicated."

"Thanks," I said. "I don't know where to start. I mean, I need a job, a place to stay first? I've never done anything like move somewhere new."

"You can work here," Jan said. "I can always use a hand."

My business brain wondered how he could afford to hire someone with such a small market, but I wasn't sure how to ask.

"Yeah, you have no idea," he said with a grin, clearly reading my mind. "Lots of the residents don't bother to cook, so I have a ton of people in here for meals. I send out a bunch, too. And I take internet orders for my other product."

"Jan makes the best ciders," D said. "He runs a subscription club every year with Lance."

"I think the value is more in the contribution from the earth witches," Lance said. "That's what makes our product the best."

I should have thought about that. I mean the world is a global marketplace, and there was no reason the witches couldn't export to the normal world.

"I'm a lousy waitress," I said.

"You can get a few hours in with me," Lilibeth said. "I kennel some animals when people travel. They always need someone to exercise them, or just talk to them sometimes."

"Are they familiars?" I asked. "How do I find one of my own?"

"Some are pets, but familiars are hard to travel with," she said. "It's not like a raven can be a comfort animal. But you don't find yours, they find you."

That was disappointing. "Thanks for the offer, but I was hoping to make my own business. How would that work?"

"The council will need to approve your plan," Jan said.

"D here can help you set up, and all of us can help with the paperwork. What did you have in mind?"

"I want to get a closer look at the meditation tents," I said. "I think it would be a perfect place to run retreats."

"For?" Lilibeth asked. "You can't bring normals here."

"Other communities," I said, the idea taking shape as I talked. "Would that make sense? Or is that allowed? A small group from, say, the mainland?"

"You'll have to think it through. We do have other witches come to visit. Not exactly a tourist season, but it's a precedent. And we'd all benefit from some new faces," Lance said. "Just witches, or shifters, too?"

"I don't know. I guess the first thing is to look at the tents and see what needs to be done."

L ilibeth took me to her shop after lunch. I tried not to hope too much that a darling cat would tell me he or she was my familiar, but I wasn't successful.

Inside wasn't what I expected, a bunch of cages and pens to hold the animals in check and out of the food supplies. Lilibeth led me into what was basically an open space where the animals ran loose. There were no shelves of food or toys, or adorable little outfits. Just a comfy chair, currently draped with two cats, and a desk.

"Off, ladies," Lilibeth said to the cats, and they stretched and then jumped down. "Take the chair. We'll see how the residents take to you."

I sat and tried to take inventory. I didn't want to ask too many stupid and possibly offensive questions. There were six dogs, four of them puppies, none of them the same breed. A pile of kittens slept in the corner, and four adult cats, at least that's what I could see. Perhaps others were hiding in the cat condo. Birds perched everywhere. The animals had one thing in common: they stared at me like they'd never seen anyone like me before.

"Is this normal?" I asked.

"They don't get to see many newcomers," Lilibeth said. "Anyone seem more interested?"

None of the animals moved toward me, and I had no idea how to read their body language. I tried to keep the disappointment out of my voice. "No. Should I be doing anything?"

She shrugged. "I can't talk to them, just sense what they need."

"No, she doesn't listen." The voice seemed to be in my head. Lilibeth hadn't reacted at all. Was I going mad? Was this my power?

"Who said that?" I said it out loud rather than think it. If I was going crazy, it was best to know sooner than later.

"Said what?" Lilibeth said.

"It was in my head," I said. "Someone doesn't think you listen."

She smiled widely. "You can hear them, that's great. They can't or won't distinguish between me not hearing them and not wanting to."

"Does that mean I'll take one of them?" A cat, please be a cat!

"I don't talk to them, remember?" She opened the back door and the animals all rushed outside. "They can be tricksters. You'll have to be patient. And we can talk to Phillip, he'll have a book on animal conversation. But right now, do you want to check out the tents? Or wait until tomorrow?"

"You can just leave? Won't they all start fighting?" I nodded toward the backyard.

"No. They're all content, and here on Henbane, the animals seem to work together even if they don't have magic. There are wards to keep the raptors out and soften the weather. They'll be fine until dinner. Just enough time for us to go peek at your new business."

"So, you think it will be a good idea?" I followed her out the door and toward the bikes.

"I do, but you need the council to agree," she said. "Grab a bike and wait here."

She headed toward the back of the parking lot. What do you call a place to park your bike?

Lilibeth returned in a few seconds wheeling a rainbow-painted bike and wearing a matching helmet. "You can customize yours when you buy one," she said after seeing my expression.

"I can't wait. How do I get the council to agree? And I guess is there a small business loan available?" I had so many other questions, but I'd have to save my breath for riding. Lilibeth kept up a much faster pace than Phillip.

IT TOOK LESS than a half hour to get to the tents. Up close I could see they needed a bit of TLC to make them welcoming, but the basics looked good. Solid roofs, windows dirty but intact, and doors locked. Small enough for one person but still big enough to hold up to three if they didn't mind being cozy.

"If you built a common room kind of space, people could bunk here too," Lilibeth said. "Use the tents for meditation and spell work, and then the bigger building could have bunk beds, a kitchen and a bathroom."

It would take some time, but she was right. This wasn't some tourist destination with hotels and B&Bs all over the place. "Do you know what's inside?" I asked. "It would give me a better idea of what's needed or possible for the business plan."

She touched the door handle of the closest tent, or cabin, or whatever the name was for a tent-cabin hybrid and mumbled some words. I heard a musical tone, like someone had struck a steel drum. She opened the door and stood back. "Give it a minute to freshen."

From somewhere a breeze whirled through the door and then back out, carrying a few leaves.

"Ready?" Lilibeth asked.

We stepped inside. It was darker than I expected. The dirt on the windows did a great job of blocking the afternoon sun. What I could see was a round space with a bench circling the wall from one side of the door to the other, with a pit in the center. There were shelves set on the wall randomly, all empty.

"Is it okay to use my phone for light?"

"You have so much to learn," Lilibeth said. "Technology has no effect on magic, and vice versa. Go ahead."

I had everything to learn. I activated the flashlight and looked more clearly. There was room to put a cot if someone needed to stay, but it wouldn't be comfortable for more than a night or two. The pit in the center was shallow, and there were holes around the edge. I turned to ask Lilibeth what they were for when the light hit the bottom of the pit. I screamed.

There was a dead woman curled up in the center. I knew she was dead, because her face was half-buried in the ashes from an old fire.

"We need to wait outside," Lilibeth said. Her voice sounded calm, but when I looked at her, I could see shock, and her hand was trembling as she pointed outside. "I'll call Mark."

I followed instructions and waited while she made the call before asking the obvious question. "Who is Mark?"

"Our police. He's never had to deal with murder, but this could be an accident," she said. "It has to be an accident. If not, someone on the island committed murder."

I wasn't as sure as Lilibeth about the cause. I'd seen the hole in the woman's head. It looked very much like she'd been attacked. "What kind of accident? I mean, she looks like she was placed in the pit."

Lilibeth walked away from me toward our bikes. "Maybe a ritual," she said. "Wait over here with me. Mark won't be long."

Unless he had access to some kind of vehicle, he wouldn't get here soon. "Do you know her?"

"I don't know everyone on the island. There's a village of earth witches on the point and the shifters on the other side.

Both communities have people who mix with the main witches, but more of them keep to themselves. And the solitaries are scattered through the island, and don't come to the village much. I know a couple of relatives are visiting this week." She was rambling, and I could feel her panic building.

"Okay. Let's not talk about it. Tell me more about the island. It will keep your mind off what we found."

"Do you think she was killed today?" Lilibeth asked, ignoring my attempt to redirect her to a safe topic.

"If this was anywhere else, I would say maybe. I mean, she wasn't bloated, or all dried up, or half-eaten by insects. Is there a spell that could preserve her?" It occurred to me that my arrival and the discovery of the body wouldn't help me settle in.

"I don't know. We don't study each other's disciplines in depth. Mark will interview people. I'm sure he'll ask."

"Then we wait," I said. I made another attempt to change the topic. I knew it was hard with the body only steps away, but panic wasn't going to help us find the answers we needed. Answers I needed, I guess. If Henbane Island was to be my new home, I didn't want any suspicion to get in the way of finding my place here. "Why do the earth witches stay separate?"

"Here he is," Lilibeth said. "Mark will know what to do."

MARK TURNED out to be a guy not much older than me, well-built, a good head taller than either of us, and serious looking, but that could be the scar that ran down his left cheek, or maybe the dead body he'd come to see. He got off his bike and joined us. Pulling out a notebook and starting with Lilibeth, he got our story.

"What did you touch?" he asked. "You're the new girl, right?"

I nodded, trying to remember all the advice I'd heard on cop shows. The one that kept rising to the top was not to talk without a lawyer.

"I should let you know I can tell when people lie to me," he said.

"I opened the door," Lilibeth said. "We went inside and then Cossi found the body. I don't remember touching anything."

He kept his eyes on me while he made notes. "Cossi?"

"I didn't. Like Lilibeth said, we went in and just looked around. Then I saw the body. Shouldn't you be looking at it, calling in some forensic team?"

"It's not the mundane world," he said. "I'll check it out. The doctor will do the autopsy if needed."

"Do you need anything more from us?" Lilibeth asked.

"You can go home," he said. "Ms. Fortuna, you're staying with Phillip, right? Over the bookstore?"

"Until I can find a place, yes."

"Don't go finding a place without telling me," he said.

He wrote in his notebook again, then turned to the tent. It was like we'd been dismissed. Lilibeth was relieved. I could feel it rolling off her in waves. Her panic subsided, and all she wanted was to return to her animals. I'd never felt anyone's emotions so clearly as I did hers. Something about the situation, or the island was changing me.

"Are you going in there by yourself?" I asked. "Don't you need backup?"

Lilibeth tugged my arm. "He knows what to do. Let's get back."

Okay, so I get that my experience was all Hollywood-based, but it didn't feel right at all that one cop was going into the crime scene. What stops him from planting evidence? Or screwing something up?

"What are you suggesting?" Mark asked me. "You don't know how we work here, so keep your suspicions to yourself until you learn."

Well, that was the least subtle dismissal I could imagine. He wasn't as confident as his words presented. Inside, he was worried. He didn't think he could handle it. Should I say something reassuring? Or maybe do as he said?

"Fine," I said. "It's getting late. I have things to learn."

11

There was nothing to do but agree to let Mark do his thing. I wasn't an investigator, and I had plenty of other things to take my time, like fitting in, not making big mistakes, and finding a way to contribute. Despite the dead body, I still wanted to explore the idea of meditation retreats at the tents.

Lilibeth calmed down as soon as we got back to the pet store. It might have had something to do with the way the animals snuggled up to her when she let them inside. I certainly didn't get snuggles. I got nasty remarks about upsetting their human. Great.

"Go get changed," Lilibeth said. "We're eating at Jan's place again."

Food should have been the last thing on my mind, but I was hungry. Pedaling around the island burned calories, I guess.

"I'll see you later," I said. Having a job was even more important if I ate every meal in the cafe. I didn't want to keep racking up debt, but there was nothing I could do about it today.

. . .

WHEN I WALKED into A Bite and a Sip, I saw the same people waiting for me at a table near the counter. Only two more tables were occupied. And everyone in the room was around my age.

D looked up as I joined the table. "Lilibeth was just telling us what happened," he said. "You don't come in quiet, do you? Our first murder on your first day."

I sighed and pulled out a chair. I had hoped these people wouldn't blame me. I ordered a beer and picked up the menu. "I don't think the two events are connected."

"You don't smell like someone who just killed," Lance said. "Don't let anyone pretend we haven't had problems before you got here."

Jan put my beer down on the table and suggested the chicken burger. "The cop didn't seem to think it was murder," I said.

"Mark? He got the job because of his powers. He got his powers from his dad, the last cop." D didn't seem overly impressed.

"I'm sure he'll do fine," Lilibeth said. "Can we talk about something else, please?"

Fine with me, that's all I wanted to do. "Will this mean I can't continue with the idea of running a business there?"

"Like it's cursed ground?" D said. He grinned at me. "Nope. Mark will release it as soon as the doctor has checked it out. It's not like the normals. He'll set a spell to stop people from entering the scene for a while. But it will be freed up soon. You still want to do a meditation retreat? You probably want to do a cleansing before you open."

It seemed like everyone knew everything and I knew nothing. "I think I should get to know the people here, first,"

I said. "I don't want to be the ignorant in-comer any longer than I need to."

"We'll answer all your questions," Jan said. He placed my food on the table and sat at the empty seat across from Lilibeth. "What's the first?"

Oh, I wasn't that organized, but something was poking at my curiosity. "Is Phillip the only older person on the island?"

"Not at all," D said. "We just kind of gravitate to Jan's. The older witches eat at home, or in the other cafe. Food for Us caters to more traditional tastes."

Jan moved to take an order from another table.

"So, who do I need to meet? I mean for fitting in, but also to learn about the island. And my parents." The last was said a little more quietly.

"Phillip will set you up with some people to teach you," Lance said. "You might want to hold off on asking about your parents. It's a tricky subject for the elders."

"So, you did come," a woman spoke, the voice a little scratchy and old.

I hadn't noticed her enter, and by the look on everyone's faces, she was a surprise to them too. She was bent over, and I'd guess her age to be somewhere around a hundred and fifty years old, if witches lived that long. She wore a shapeless black dress and thick boots. Her gray hair was pulled into a bun on top of her head.

Jan stepped beside her. "Mrs. Vestum, a pleasure to see you here."

"Don't try to soft soap me, Jan Mikelson. I knew you before you were born."

"I'm sure you knew most of us the same way," he said. "Can I offer you a tea or something stronger?"

"That girl is trouble. The minute she arrived, we have a

violent death. I suspect she's trying to finish what her mother started. I will not have it." She turned and limped toward the door, mumbling under her breath.

"I'm sorry," Jan said. "Cossi, she's only one voice on the council. And not everyone agrees with her."

So, some people did. Should I have listened to Dad and avoided this place?

12

By the end of the day, I had two part-time jobs, both felt like pity hires, but what's a desperate witch to do? I wasn't going to be able to live on the income even if I stayed above the bookstore, but I wouldn't be a charity case. Between the time with Jan and Lilibeth, Phillip promised me a few hours working at the bookstore.

I SLEPT through without any nightmares about women being killed. Or, at least, none I remembered. My first job was with Lilibeth, and being around a bunch of pets who were pissed at you was probably not great when you didn't have to listen to the complaints. But for me it was a litany of mistakes.

"Brush me with the other one," a puppy said. Since Lilibeth had given me the tool, I took it as a personal jab.

"Look, everyone," I said after trying to ignore them for an hour, "I've never been allowed to have a pet. If you won't choose to be my familiar, why are you talking to me?"

A parrot dropped from the top shelf to land on my

shoulder. "You upset Lilibeth yesterday. We like her; we don't know you."

At least someone was willing to tell the truth. "The body upset her. And it upset me too."

The parrot cawked and ruffled her feathers, almost toppling me over.

"You never use our names," the parrot said. "We are just animals to you."

"You never told me your names," I said. "I'm Cossi." I didn't know if I was supposed to add anything.

"Clara," the parrot said. "You won't remember all the names, but that puppy is Joshua, the kittens haven't chosen names yet. Learn three a day."

"Thank you, Clara." I finished brushing Joshua and went to find Lilibeth.

She was sitting at her computer, entering what looked like invoices. "What's next?" I asked.

"Oh, you've fed, watered, and groomed everyone? I was so focused on this paperwork that I didn't notice time passed."

"I guess all businesses have admin," I said. "If I want to set up, is there anything special for here?" I knew everything to do in the mundane world, thanks to my education. But a secret island full of magical people wasn't part of the curriculum.

"Same as everywhere. You just need approval. If you want to use the tents, I guess you'll need to wait for Mark to clear the scene. And get the owner's approval — that's the council, too.

"Will they approve me? Mrs. Vestum didn't seem too happy I was here."

"You'll need a majority. And she doesn't control more than two members. A good business case will stop her from blocking you. I mean, you need to contribute, and that means working. People will want you to be independent."

I hoped independent didn't mean working a bunch of part-time jobs forever. In fact, I should probably also look at an exit strategy from Henbane. I'd made friends here, or at least started to, but I couldn't stick around where I wasn't wanted. I had the spell for reaching out to a new community. I could get the herbs easily, and Philip's apartment had a fireplace.

"What about marketing, equipment, taxes, all the other stuff running a business entails?" I asked.

"We have a person for each of those, and we all use the house in Sechelt as an address for the business. Focus on getting approval and the rest will fall into place."

I didn't care for that idea. I liked to plan out everything. I would get the approval. I would make a success of the business. I was going to stay here. I would find out what happened to force my parents to flee.

And I wouldn't make an exit strategy because I wasn't going to fail.

"I have to head over to the bookstore," I said. "Will I see you at the cafe for dinner?"

She turned back to the computer. "Actually, why don't we go to the bar? You can meet some of the shifters."

13

My nerves were in shreds thinking of entering a bar full of werewolves, but I kept it all inside. Lilibeth didn't seem worried, and Lance had seemed in control of the animal he'd turn into, so I was likely just reacting to all the stories I'd read. And I didn't want to come across as an idiot. Logic said the island was safe and so the shifters must be okay. Logic didn't make a dent in my emotions.

"I guess it's okay to have a few drinks," I said. "Cycling while drunk isn't illegal or dangerous to anyone else, right?"

"No one will serve you enough to get you fall-down drunk," Lilibeth said. "Mark doesn't want to deal with a bunch of injuries from people crashing their bikes, and no one wants to send people to the mainland hospital for something so stupid. One of the transport buggies will bring you home if you can't ride or walk."

We rounded a corner in the path and suddenly there was a whole community laid out. The hills weren't very high, but it was enough to keep the shifter village hidden up to this point.

"Wow, I wasn't expecting this," I said.

"What did you expect?" Lilibeth asked.

"I'm not sure, but something smaller?" She didn't respond, and I felt like a tourist for commenting.

The bar was at the very front of the village, a large neon sign with a stein of beer shone from the roof. Behind it, three streets ran parallel to the water, each with houses in the middle of wide lots lined up. Then there were lights randomly shining from places in the surrounding hills. If there were only about two thousand people on Henbane, at least five hundred of them had to be shifters.

We rode to the small parking lot and left our bikes leaning against a split log fence. "Is there anything I should know before we go in?" I asked. "So I don't make any mistakes."

"I don't really know what normals think of shifters," Lilibeth said. "Is it anything like the books?"

"Depends on the book and the person," I said. "Mostly no one believes in them."

"They're normal people. They can control when they shift, not like in your horror stories."

Was I making up problems by trying to not upset anyone? Over thinking, my specialty. "Okay, then. What kind of beer do they serve?"

"Sheena always has something special. Just relax."

Inside, it was like I'd walked into some kind of fantasy bar. Almost everything was wood. The bar was a solid slab of some kind of dark tree, and the tables and chairs were all cedar. The place smelled like furniture wax, beer, and something meaty stewing. I felt the tension leave my shoulders as if there was a spell of welcome and comfort laid on the place.

"Cossi, Lilibeth," Lance called from behind the bar. "Come sit up here and talk to me."

He glanced around the room as he spoke, meeting the gaze of a few younger patrons. It felt like he was warning them off, but not like he was trying to monopolize us.

"Try this," he said, placing two mugs of beer in front of us. "Sheena is giving fruit beer a try."

I sniffed before I tasted, having disliked the fruit-flavored beers I'd tried in the past. They all tasted to me like beer that had been sprayed with furniture polish. This one was different. I inhaled hops, wheat, and a warm aroma of plums. I sipped and it tasted the same as it smelled. "It's perfect."

"Thanks, I'm pretty proud of it. Not all the experiments worked." The woman who spoke stepped in from the kitchen in the back. Raven hair, dark eyes, and a face that might have been sculpted by Michelangelo. She could have been a movie star. "I'm Sheena Lobo, you're the new girl."

"I guess that's a good way to describe me," I said. "My parents came from here."

"I wouldn't keep reminding people of that," she said. "Are you sticking around, or just checking us out?"

"I plan to stay," I said. "If I can get permission, I plan to open a meditation center up at the tents."

"The body must have put a hole in that plan. Mark says it's going to be a while before he can get it sorted."

If he was going to slow walk the investigation, I would be stuck racking up debt and living with Phillip for months. "Is he the right person to investigate?"

Lilibeth elbowed me like I'd said something wrong. "He can figure it out. We don't have many options. But Mark is a good guy."

"Heard it was murder," Lance said. "Someone bashed

her on the head. Dumped her body in the tent. Not enough blood on site for it to be the place she was killed."

"Do you know who it is?" There was nothing secret here, apparently.

"Leanne Macy. Her husband reported her missing, but Doc Rene recognized her. Surprised Mark didn't," Lance said.

"I don't think any of us got a clear look," Lilibeth said. "Weird. I knew it had to be someone on the island, but now we know who, it feels worse. Poor Peter."

I couldn't rely on my site being available if no one had experience with murders.

"You need someone with you," Sheena said.

I looked at her. Had I said something out loud? "Where?"

"Sorry, it's what I do. You are going to look into the murder. I can't tell if you'll be successful. But you can't go alone. You need to take Lance."

14

The next day I met Lance at the tent where we'd found Mrs. Macy. I'd been suspicious of Sheena's prediction, but Lilibeth assured me that it was real. Apparently, she didn't always see the future, but when she did, everything happened as she predicted it. So if I decided to go along, or not go, or any number of other choices, I'd still find myself standing next to Lance facing the tent where I'd found the body.

There was no police tape or seal to worry about. No one stood guard to keep us out. All of which reinforced my belief that Mark wasn't up to the job. Even if I felt guilty about my assumption when I didn't know the guy.

"Ready?" Lance asked. "I have the spell to open the door. You have any idea what we're looking for?"

I had no plan whatsoever. "I think just looking around will help," I said. "I have no idea if I have the right kind of magic, and I've never done this before. It just feels like I found the body, so I should find the killer to make up for it."

"People have been hassling you?"

"Only one person overtly. I just feel like everyone is judging me for something I didn't do." The feeling had followed me all morning as I worked the bookstore shift. It wasn't that I carried any guilt. It was like I'd walked into a room where people were talking about me and then they stopped.

"Stick around and prove yourself, and people will forget what your mother did. What are your powers?"

"I can hear animals. That's all I know. Is there more?" We were wasting time, but I couldn't help thinking if we rushed in, I'd do the wrong thing.

"We all have three powers. I can't believe your parents didn't tell you this. I'm a garden witch mostly. I manage some of the farms. D's parents trust me to take care of their place while they are gone, but don't need me when they're home."

There was a bit of resentment there. "Garden witch?"

"I can grow just about anything anywhere. I can fix anything made of natural materials. Like most of Sheena's bar. Just with magic, I don't have any skills as a carpenter — can't actually make a thing, just fix it."

I got the impression he wanted to learn to make things. "And the third?"

"It's a shifter thing, you don't need to know about it."

And with that, the door into his personality slammed shut. "So, how do I find out what my other two powers are? Will they be about animals?"

"Phillip might be able to test you. There are plenty of books you can study in his store."

So, he didn't want to get involved. I guess that was understandable since we'd only met a few days ago.

"Let's go in," I said. "Maybe I can find a mouse to ask." I laughed at the idea, but Lance nodded. It was going to take a lot of effort for me to get my mind around this whole magic thing.

Lance touched the lock and muttered a few words. The door opened, and I could see inside the tent. Nothing looked different, but then, I couldn't see inside the pit from here.

"We don't have much time," Lance said. "There was a notification on the seal. Mark will be here as soon as he can be."

I stepped inside and waited for Lance to join me. This time I didn't look for business potential, I checked the interior against my memory. It all seemed to be the same. "I can't see anything like a clue," I said.

"Look in the pit," he said. "I meant it when I said we don't have much time. I can smell death, blood, and something bitter. All a few days old. I think this happened just before you arrived."

At least that was something in my favor. I couldn't be a suspect. I was being evicted at the time of the murder.

I tiptoed to the edge of the pit. No body, thank goodness. "It's been cleared out," I said. "No sign of the ashes or anything else that was there when I found her."

"The bitterness is rue," Lance said. He sniffed deeply, held the breath and then let it out slowly, sticking his tongue out to catch the air. "Yes. Rue and daffodil. Repentance and forgiveness."

15

"What are you doing here?" Mark had arrived, and he wasn't happy with finding us standing outside his murder scene.

"I want to set up a business," I said. "There's no crime scene tape or anything to indicate I shouldn't be doing my research. If you want people to stay away, you should make it clear."

It was true, because if I didn't get this murder solved, I'd never get the business started. It was also not the whole truth, and I could tell he knew.

"I'm taking care of this," he said. "I don't need anyone getting in the way. No matter how pretty they are."

"You think I'm pretty? Or that I don't matter?" I was absurdly pleased with the first comment. I had no time for a relationship, and I figured that a quick fling would make me a subject of gossip. Small island, small town. It didn't matter about the magic. People were people, and no matter how broody and intense this guy was, I'd steer clear.

"Look, I can tell when you're lying. It's what makes me a

good cop. So, don't pretend you were here for anything other than trying to beat me to solving this case."

I didn't want to comment on him passing over the answers to my questions. I needed him at least not mad at me every time he saw me. I looked to Lance for help with handling Mark, but he was gone.

"Yeah, Lance got scarce. You're on your own with me."

I refused to speak because he hadn't asked a question. I was well trained from TV shows that babbling was a sure way to get yourself arrested, even if you were innocent.

He looked over my shoulder at the open door of the tent. Then he focused on me again as if trying to read my mind, and maybe he could. It would be nice to know what powers all the people I knew had. Was there a registry? I'd get right on that after I got permission to start my business, and figured out my own powers, and made peace with the animals in Lilibeth's shop, and, and, and...

"Did you find anything?"

"You mean, anything you missed? How should I know?"

"No, I meant, did you and Lance find anything? I'm not telling you details of the investigation. Maybe I'm already aware of the facts, but you, as an outsider, would have a different interpretation."

It felt like he was making an effort, although unlike most of the people I met, I had no idea how to read him. "Lance noticed the scent of rue and daffodil. I don't know what that means, and you scared him off."

"I didn't scare Lance off. He's a busy guy, and I know where to find him. Rue and daffodil have uses like most plants, and they symbolize things for potion makers."

"What?"

"You work in the bookstore, look them up." He stepped behind me to close the door and set the spell to lock it.

"Do you have a suspect?" It was worth asking even if I didn't know anyone outside the few people I'd met.

"Not yet. I spoke to her husband. I'm waiting for the doctor to report on the autopsy and tox reports."

"You have a lab here?" That was a surprise, especially since everyone made a big deal about this being the only murder ever to happen.

"No. We send samples to the mainland for the usual screening. One of the earth witches here will do tests for magical poisons." He snapped his mouth shut.

"Is there anything else? I would really like to help. Not just because I have plans here, but don't cops work in teams?"

I could see him fighting the urge to tell me. Maybe one of my talents was forcing people to answer me. I didn't like the forcing bit of that, but it would really help for getting settled.

"Enough. I don't need your help." He swallowed and seemed to regret the roughness of his words. "You went to Sheena's place yesterday."

"Are you watching me?"

He flushed. "No. I was wondering if we could meet for a drink."

"A date?"

"Yes."

"What will we talk about if we can't discuss the murder?"

"We'll find something. It's just a date. I can give you some of the history, point you in the right direction for settling in."

I didn't know if he was my type because I hadn't dated enough to know the kind of guy I connected with best. And I had no idea what the social conventions were, or the size of the dating pool. It was only day three of my new life.

"I'll think about it," I said. "Right now we both have higher priorities."

16

"D is here," Phillip said as soon as I entered our apartment. "I'll bring refreshments."

D sat at the dining table with a laptop and note pad in front of him. "I thought we could get started on the list of actions required to set up a business."

My mind wasn't on red tape at the moment. I was trying to process the fact that Mark could be so much of a block to my investigation and still want to go on a date. "Oh, great. I thought that might not be cool to do right now. With the murder being so fresh. I mean, don't get me wrong. I'm eager, but isn't it in bad taste?"

He laughed and patted the seat next to him. "You won't be meeting anyone for a while. At least let me give you the checklist and contacts."

"I'll work in the store for a couple of hours," Phillip said. He deposited a tray of tea and cookies on the table and left us.

D patted the seat again and looked at me, a smile on his face. He reminded me of the guys I went to university with. More accurately, he reminded me of two kinds of guys. The nerds who were excited about tiny details of the back end of business, and the jocks who took the degree because they thought it would be an easy pass. D was pale, like he didn't get out much, or was genetically predisposed to sunburn, but he had the body of a tennis player. And no nerd I met was ever this comfortable around other people.

"Can I ask you some questions first? About how the island works. And the people and the... I don't know, social norms, if that's not too woke."

"Didn't Phillip give you the talk?"

"The talk? Like don't get into strange cars, or agree to go to a second location?"

He laughed aloud. "I guess everyone has a different definition of 'the talk'. No. He should have told you all about the island. At a high level, I guess. You haven't been around long enough for him to get into the details."

Was that what he was doing in the house when we first met? "I guess he told me the rules, but really just high level."

"We don't get many people joining us," D said, "and none that don't know the usual magic conventions." He closed the laptop, took a cookie and gestured for me to start talking.

He was so much easier to read than Mark. D wanted to help me. He didn't have anything to hide, but he wasn't investigating a serious crime or asking me out. His job was to help.

So where did I start? I couldn't just ask him outright to help me find the killer. "Powers. I get that everyone has three, but is it rude to talk about them? Like, can I ask what power someone has?"

"We don't usually need to ask. I guess it's okay to ask the people you know, but I wouldn't go around asking everyone. It will look like you're up to something. And with your mother's past, the older ones are going to think it's to expose the island."

I would eventually make my own mark here, but it was useful to know not everyone would look for ulterior motives. "So what are yours?"

"I can fix any problem with technology. It's like I can talk to devices and cure them. I like that. Devices have no emotional baggage. I can read the weather, so that makes me useful for the farmers. If I know some bad front is coming, I can soften the blow or redirect it. Takes days for me to recover, but it's worth it."

Controlling the weather was a huge thing now. I wondered if he could do something about climate change. But that was too huge, probably. "Can you tell what mine are?"

"No. Phillip will help you find them. I've never heard of anyone who didn't know from just after birth what they could do. Has anything changed?"

"I can hear animals talk."

"What about other languages?"

"Everyone here speaks English. I don't remember understanding anyone around me speaking anything but that."

"Sometimes the power to hear animals is just confined to that, and sometimes it's just that you understand language."

Why didn't he just tell me what I needed to hear and stop hinting around it? "How will I know if everyone here speaks the same language as me?"

"I just told you that in Farsi. So..."

Oh my goodness. "So can I speak another language the same way as I hear them?"

"Do you speak one?"

"A bit of French."

"Don't we all. Something to test later. What else?"

"I haven't noticed anything."

"Okay. Phillip should test you on a bunch of things. He'll start with the powers your parents had and branch out. So, you want to start making lists of tasks?"

No. I had a much more interesting idea. "What do you know about plant symbols?"

17

"Are you thinking about studying potions and cures?" D asked. "Or hexes? I wouldn't recommend that as a starting point."

"No, the thought of mixing up spells and making a mistake doesn't appeal. I'm sure there are way too many opportunities to get everything wrong. I was up at the murder scene with Lance, and he sniffed out rue and daffodil. I thought it might be a clue."

"Let Mark investigate," D said. "You have more important things on your plate right now. Like learning about Henbane and your powers, and your business."

"Not if the tents stay off limits," I said. "I don't think I would be good at much else here, and I need to start generating income. I promise I'll do both, right? You can help me solve the case, and you can show me how to get my business set up."

I stopped talking because something in his expression told me I was pushing too hard. Weirdly I read it as concern rather than frustration.

Also weird that I didn't question my interpretation. I

guess too many new things put me off balance and it was starting to feel normal to be off kilter — or overwhelmed or freaked out.

"Cossi, you can't go forcing yourself on everything. Remember, Mrs. Vestum is not the only person who blames your mother for the disaster. You don't need anyone switching sides."

"I'm not here to create problems," I said. He looked away like he could hide his emotions from me. "Sorry. I know you are trying to be helpful, but I'm not my mother. I can't do anything about the Mrs. Vestums of this place. Not until I prove myself and contribute to the island's wellbeing or give them something else to worry about."

He looked back at me. "I'll help, but you need to promise me three things."

Three seemed a powerful number here. "What?"

"You'll stop investigating if it gets dangerous. I know you're used to things like murder being from the mainland, but we aren't. We all have the same kinds of problems, but with such a small community, someone always steps in before anything goes too far. This murder means that we missed all the clues. And the killer could come after you. I would hate for you to get killed just when we're getting to know each other."

I hadn't thought of it that way. "I promise. I have no intention of being the next victim. I have no idea who might be angry enough to kill someone. But I'm stuck until the murder is solved. What else do you want me to promise?"

"You'll do the work to identify your powers." He stared at me this time, like he was putting a spell on me.

"No kidding. I can't wait for that."

"You will make it a priority to get set up here. Even if it sounds wrong, or weird."

"Yes. I promise, even though I expect everything to sound weird. Is that all?"

"Yes. For now." He pulled his laptop between us. "You can read over my shoulder."

He pulled up a spreadsheet filled with names. "This is the resident list," he said. "There are too many people who would know about the plants to narrow down. The Macys own Sweet and Bitter, the tea and potions shop. Mark has Peter down as the top suspect."

"How do you know that?" Was I talking to the wrong person? Was D going to tell Mark what I was doing?

"Mark asked me to set up a confidential folder he could use. I entered the first few notes." He held up a hand to stop me asking the next question. "That's all it is for now. Maybe he's right, but as I understand it, the husband is often the first suspect, but not always the actual killer. And I won't hack into Mark's folder for you."

"It wouldn't help," I said. "My plan is to find the killer, not follow Mark around." Not sure when I'd made it a competition. Possibly when he asked me out?

He nodded acceptance and then typed in another query. "Pretty much everyone on the island could look up the uses of plants. There's no point in trying to figure out who bought them because the earth witches would just grow them, and they wouldn't know who might have taken a few samples."

"Are they poisonous? I know she was bashed on the head, but could the plants be what actually killed her?"

"Cause of death was the head wound. All plants can be poisonous at the right strength, but these two are known for meaning forgiveness and repentance, among other things. I'd put money on the killer regretting what happened and leaving these as messages."

"Maybe a crime of passion?"

"Yes, but that doesn't point to anyone in particular. Is there another search I can do? Or can we go back to setting up your business?"

"One question, but it's not about the case." Mainly because I couldn't think of another question, not because I'd given up. "Is there some record of powers?"

"You'll find a dictionary of talents in Phillip's store. He'll do some testing to help you know exactly what you are blessed with. We know you can understand languages, but there are many facets of language power."

"I will talk to him. I just feel like I'm missing something just thinking everyone has magic powers. If I can research what that means, I'll feel more like I fit in."

"Okay. Look, I have another half hour, let's go through the basics of what to do first on your business."

By the time he had to leave, I learned that there was a giant proposal just for the council. The good thing was it contained all the steps to get a business license and a business loan. The loan would come from the council too, but they wouldn't play games like giving me the license and then turning down my loan application.

That wasn't the only game, though. If they really wanted to mess with me, the council could make me apply for approval multiple times, finding little nitpicky issues each submission. I needed to make friends on that council.

18

I didn't get a chance to do anything that day. Phillip made me dinner and we talked about the island in general. Every time I asked for something specific, he changed the subject. Nothing suspicious, he claimed I needed to digest my new life in small pieces. He did say he was on the council, which meant I had an ally.

I got up the next morning and did my shifts with Lilibeth and Jan before I tried to figure out my next steps. I had two giant goals. One was to get myself settled and start a business. The other was to solve the murder so I could carry on with the first goal.

Thinking about it that way made me realize I had them in the wrong order. Yes, there was plenty I needed to do before I could open my meditation center, but if the crime remained unsolved, I would never get to opening day. Mark might be the best cop on the island — as far as I could tell, he was the only one, but I probably had more experience in real crime just by living in a city.

I learned that the police station didn't exist. Mark worked out of his home most of the time. A place just off

Main Street behind Phillip's shop. I'd forgotten to look up his phone number, so I was going to have to take a chance. I got two coffees from Jan and headed to the address.

The house was a bungalow, designed in that California architectural style that was all straight lines. I wondered if he had a spell to keep his roof from leaking. Flat roofs and west coast rain didn't always work well together. His place was done in creams and natural wood that fit well with the trees that lined the back of the house.

I didn't see any signs leading to a police station entrance, so I rang the doorbell and waited. If he wasn't in, I'd have to think of a way to track him — and drink the second coffee myself.

He opened the door after a few seconds. Today he was wearing something that looked more like a uniform, but there was no gun or utility belt. He still had an intense stare and, to be perfectly honest, looked really hot. Maybe that date was a good idea. Having a romantic life hadn't even hit my list of to-dos. "What can I do for you?"

I held out the coffee for him. "I think we got off to the wrong start. I brought a peace offering."

He looked at the paper cup and for a second, I thought he was going to refuse it and slam the door in my face. Then he pulled the door open wider and accepted the drink. "Office is on the right."

The inside of his house was open plan, so I could see through the patio doors to his yard. The kitchen ran along half of one wall, ending at a door that must have led to bedrooms and bathrooms. The office was just a desk, computer, single black filing cabinet and three chairs. The space was defined by a large area rug in a pattern of gray and sea foam.

I took a seat in one of the guest chairs and waited for

him to sit in his. I hadn't managed to think of a way to subtly bring up the subject of the investigation, so I just barreled in with the first question. "Have you found anything that will solve the murder?"

"I don't discuss cases with anyone."

A dog trotted into the office and sat beside my chair as if waiting for me to give him a treat, or a scratch. It looked like someone had patched together a bunch of leftover dog material and then splashed bleach on its back.

"Australian cattle breed." It was the dog talking in my head. "No one ever guesses right the first time. Name's Roy."

"He likes you," Mark said.

"Is he your familiar?" I so desperately wanted to know how to get one that I hoped Mark, or Roy, could tell me.

"No. He's a work dog. Is there anything else?"

"Did you look into the smell of the plants?" I asked.

"He did," Roy said.

"Yes, too many possibilities to narrow down the source. Earth witches grow everything in their village. Someone anywhere here could have a patch of either plant for decoration. It can even be bought off-island. It'll take more to turn that into a useful clue."

Roy put his paw on my knee, and I gave his ears a scratch. "Tell him it's from the island," Roy said.

"The plants are from the island," I said. "Roy told me."

"You can hear dogs?"

"All animals. Apparently, a bunch of languages I don't speak, too. It's hard sometimes to tune out the background."

"Well, if you get more from any of the non-human residents, let me know. I have to get back to work. Thanks for the coffee."

"I need that crime solved," I said. "I don't want to sound

selfish, but that piece of land is my future. Do you have help?"

He looked like he was going to shut me down again, but Roy barked. I heard it both in my head as 'hey', and a real bark.

"Fine. I have a mentor in another community, and a few people on the island who I can talk to. That means I don't need your help. You should focus on getting settled." He stood and led me to the door.

I didn't know what to say. I mean, if a cop spoke to me like that last week, I would have torn a strip off him. It was different now. Here, I was trying to find my place, and Mark wasn't part of a police force; it sounded like he was the police force. No date for him unless something changed. And now I knew where I got the idea it was a competition. His attitude rubbed me the wrong way.

So I pressed my lips together and walked past him without a word.

19

Nothing else happened to help me solve the case for the rest of the day. No revelations on how to get my business idea going either. After dinner at Jan's again, I settled in for an evening of reading in Phillip's store after hours so I wouldn't be disturbed.

Books on magical powers didn't read like a primer. I guess when most people knew they were witches from the start, there'd be no reason to do more than just create definitions. Parents took care of the explaining.

"How is it going?" Phillip asked. I hadn't heard him come in. The store was closed and the last thing I remember, he was upstairs with a glass of wine and a pile of paperwork.

"It's not," I said, closing the book I was scanning for 'find your powers' information. "When a kid is born here, how does anyone know what powers they have?"

"The powers tend to manifest around the seventh birthday." He sat beside me and picked up the books, checking the titles. "You'll find no help here. These are scholarly works. Give me a moment."

He pushed the books to the side and went to the children's section. I should have thought of that. Was I too proud to think kids' books would help? I'd used that algebra book for middle graders when I had to do math for my projects. So, why was I so unwilling to do the same when the help was offered?

"Here." He placed two thin books in front of me. One had a turtle on the front and the other had a purple mushroom with googly eyes. Not just kid's books. Baby books.

I flipped open the turtle one. The hero was talking to a rhino. "Are you sure this will help?"

He laughed at my expression. "Ignore the characters. This is the age we start teaching the signs of magic. That way when the powers manifest, the kids don't freak out. They use the incident to learn."

"Incident?" I pictured flying on a broomstick and wiping out. I wisely didn't verbalize that scenario.

"Enough of them qualify to make it a reasonable label," Phillip said. "My first to manifest was my ability to project images of my memories. The teacher was a little shocked to find out I'd been listening to her talk about her date."

"Embarrassing. I guess it's the same for me with the animals and languages thing. Although I was the only one around the first time. I think the neighborhood cat said something to me when I left to come here."

"Interesting. How did you react?"

"I thought it was me," I said. "You know, thinking not hearing."

"That's the difference. If you were raised here, you would have known it was the cat."

It felt like a dig at my parents for taking me away. "Well, the first time I entered Run, Fly, Slither, I realized I could hear the animals. And D spoke to me in Farsi, which I don't speak. Is it usually fast? I mean, going from not knowing you can do something to understanding it?"

"Here, and in other witch communities, yes. But try not to assume you understand your one power. There are always subtleties."

"And I'll have two other powers?" I had my whole life to dig deeper. The animal thing might come in handy for gossip, but maybe the hidden ones would help me close the murder and get my business approved.

"Have you noticed anything since arriving?" Phillip asked. He opened the mushroom book. "Things that seemed easier, or clearer?"

I glanced at the page in front of me. The mushroom was meditating with a snail on his cap. "Should I do that?" I asked. "I mean, meditate on it?"

"Yes, but not until we have a hint. Let's see how far your language power goes." He left again. This time to a glass-fronted shelf holding scrolls. He unlocked the door and slipped on a pair of cotton gloves. I saw the reverence he had for the documents he removed in the gentle way he carried them. "Please don't touch these," he said. "I'll unroll them, and you see if you can read what's there."

The first sheet was hieroglyphics. "I can't read... oh!" The meaning of the figures came into my head. "It's a record of grain deliveries. I can't read it as much as I just know what it says."

"And this?"

The second scroll was filled with simpler symbols. "An inventory of armaments."

"Have you seen Sanskrit before?"

"No. Not that I remember. Does that mean I can understand every kind of language?"

"Most likely. You can probably only write in anything

you understand, but it will take some testing to see if you can speak any."

"If I was an historian, that would come in handy," I said. "Or maybe I can learn languages easier. I mean, I don't remember much of French from high school."

"Only if you could prove what you read was truly what it said. Sorry, there is always a slight downside."

He chuckled, but I sensed a tension in it. Part of him was jealous? Weird. I'd always been good at reading people, mostly knowing when they were telling an important lie. Although I'd missed the really big one my parents told me. But what I got from Phillip was way stronger and clearer than ever before. He was jealous. And he was happy for me.

"Is one of the powers to be able to read people's emotions?"

"Not one of the powers, it comes in many forms. Is this something you've felt since coming here?"

His jealousy spiked. "It's been a bit stronger here," I said, unwilling to let him know too much. "Should I read about Mr. Turtle and Ms. Mushroom?"

"You can take them upstairs. Don't be fooled by their simplicity. There is always something to be learned."

20

"Is it normal for a case to take so long?" I asked. We were all having a drink in The Howling Place. By all, I mean me, Lilibeth, Lance, and D. I'd kinda formed a posse over the week.

We usually ate at Jan's, and I tried not to wince every time I added a bit more to the debt I was accruing. I couldn't hide in my room eating sandwiches. I needed friends, and Phillip wasn't exactly a peer. More like an uncle.

"It's not normal to have a murder case," Lance said. "Or do you mean if it was on the mainland? They have cold cases there, right? This one will get solved, Cossi. Just not overnight."

"I know but... I mean there's only so many people to interview, right? If the killer is a resident, then Mark should have finished eliminating suspects by now."

"He talked to you," Lilibeth said.

"Only because I went looking for him." He should have interviewed me and Lilibeth right away. Not just a casual chat, but a real interrogation. "What about her husband?"

"He wouldn't kill her," D said. "Mr. Macy is too kind."

"Hmm, you know that's the kind of thing they say about serial killers, right?"

"There's something you don't understand," Lance said. "Killing isn't really a witch thing. Especially one that has some magic attached. The blowback is too big a risk."

"Blowback?" Was this a Karma thing?

"It's when you do a spell to change someone's mind," Lilibeth said. "A compulsion, or I guess anything negative, or a huge spell negative or positive."

Like my mother's mistake? "Just spells? I mean, not all witches cast them, right? For some it's just magic they have." Yes, I was worried that I'd do something stupid and have to pay a big price — like Mom.

"Only spells," D said. "It's really hard to do anything dangerous with just innate magic."

"Is that why Mark's the cop? His powers?" Part of me was hoping these guys could convince me that I didn't need to worry. If Mark had the right magic, there could be a legitimate reason he was so slow to catch the murderer. I couldn't think of one, but I was new here.

Lance signaled for another round. "Yes and no. He can tell if you're lying to him, and he can find things. And I guess it's useful to be able to block people from reading you when you're trying to solve a crime. But blocking people is pretty common, and even without powers, there are spells, or just plain techniques."

This wasn't going anywhere, at least anywhere that would help me. "So if that's the case, he's in the same position as any cop. And he doesn't have help."

"Yeah, he's not the kind of guy to ask for help either," D said. I sensed something more like jealousy every time we talked about Mark. Was there a history between them I should know about? Or was I being a bad friend by reading his emotions without permission? Or another thought, was I reading that emotion more? Phillip was definitely envying something around me.

"So, if we banded together to solve the case, we would be helping?" I asked. "I can find out if any animals know what happened. You all know the inhabitants and culture. If we combined our various powers, we'll get it done in no time."

Lance took a long sip of his beer and then nodded his approval to the server. "I can't be blocked," he said. "Not easily. I can sniff out clues, and the only way to misdirect me is to use strong odors, which is just the thing to make me suspicious."

"My powers aren't much help," Lilibeth said. "But no one will know we're investigating until it's too late, right? Whoever the murderer is, they'll concentrate on confusing Mark. It's a good idea, Cossi."

"It's dangerous," D said. "Not just the killer, but Mark won't like it when he finds out. Getting on his bad side can make life hell. He'll cite you for every little infraction." Definitely a history between them.

"He's not that petty," Lilibeth said. "We'll let him take credit and he'll forgive us."

"Yeah, I wasn't finished. We won't be affected by it, but Cossi is still building her reputation," D said with a glance at me. "And I know it's not fair but, some people are waiting for her to repeat what her mother did in some way."

Valid points, but all I'd get a reputation for, if I didn't get the business going, was being a freeloader.

"Solving the crime might make up for it," I said. "One thing I do bring that no one seems to have here is an understanding of murder."

"You've been part of a murder investigation?" Lilibeth asked.

"No. But I've lived in the normal world. People get murdered there. The press report on it. And all the trials are public records when they finish. I had a project with someone who was going into criminal behavioral analysis once. We read months' worth of transcripts."

D brightened up as I talked. I hoped that meant he was on board now he knew I had skills.

"How do I get into that site?" he asked.

"I'll send you the link," I said. "Are you planning on becoming a criminal lawyer? Or a criminal?"

He laughed along with the rest of us. "No. I like data. You can never have enough."

"So we're agreed?" Lance asked. "We're teaming up to catch a murderer?"

"I guess so," Lilibeth said.

21

I decided to make my own decision about the victim's husband, Mr. Macy. He owned the tea and potions store, Sweet and Bitter, right next to Raziel's Books. The place was closed for a few days after I discovered the body, but he reopened today. Last night, we had discussed a bunch of motives and made plans. I was supposed to be reading the twenty documents D forwarded on the history of Henbane, and basics of magic. But I couldn't let go of the knowledge that most women are killed by someone who professed to love them.

I'd worked at my side jobs all day and found out that, so far, I was earning my keep, so that was a plus. It wouldn't take much for that to change when I started creating the meditation area, but the knowledge I wasn't building up a massive debt for just living here took a weight off.

Sweet and Bitter closed at five and it was already four-thirty, so I figured I'd have to make the conversation — not interrogation — quick.

There were two other customers in the store. Mrs. Vestum, who gave me a sour look of acknowledgment when the bell over the door announced my entrance. And a man in brown robes with long gray hair tied back in a braid and six silver hoops in the ear I could see. He also held a long, crooked branch like a staff, and when he turned to glance my way, I saw a tattoo on his cheek with the moon phases. The first person I'd seen here who actually looked like a witch.

"You are the new one," he said in a warm voice that was just short of baritone. "Welcome. I hope your life is blessed."

"She is already a problem, Billy Fern. You remember her mother," Mrs. Vestum said in her creaky old witch voice.

"Cossi Fortuna," I said to Billy, holding out my hand. "Pleased to meet you. I'm still getting to know my way around."

He shook my hand and then placed a small handwoven sack in my palm. "Wear this and you will find more peace than trouble."

Mrs. Vestum snorted her disapproval and marched over to the cash register. "I'll take this, Peter."

"You can just call the store and I'll deliver," Peter said. "It's not a problem."

This was the husband. He was tall and thin with pointed features and the fingers of a pianist. I tried to push the image of a praying mantis out of my mind, but it was persistent.

I thanked Mr. Fern and looked at the various bottles and boxes on the shelves until Mrs. Vestum stomped through the door to the street. She was nasty enough to kill someone with a glance, but a tiny ancient woman could never have taken down a woman in her prime.

Although, she could have hired someone. Her name went on a new mental list of suspects I dubbed 'probably not, but don't forget them'.

"I'll be with you in a moment," Mr. Macy said, then turned to help Mr. Fern, who was selling ingredients.

"How can I help?" Mr. Macy asked, grabbing my attention from reading the ingredients on a bottle labeled Taming the Heart.

Mr. Fern had slipped out while my focus was on finding potential poisons.

"I wanted to express my condolences," I said, watching his reaction.

"Thank you. It was a shock, but I'm trying to process my grief."

"Yes, it's hard. I lost my dad not that long before I moved here. I guess with all the changes, I haven't had time to work through any of it either." Or my anger at him was getting in the way.

My read of his emotions was weak. Not like it was blocked, but maybe it was the other way around. He'd stifled his emotions for a while. But I didn't get a murder vibe, so that was something.

"Has there been any news from the investigation?" I'd hoped to be more subtle, but what can I say?

"Mark interviewed me when he came to give me the news." He leaned in like he was about to share a secret. "It was very difficult for me, but I do trust him to know his job."

"I get it," I said. "You must have found it hard to remember where you were. Shock can do all kinds of things to a person's memory."

"Indeed. Was there anything else I can help you with?"

"Maybe," I said. There was still no hint from my power that he was lying or hiding anything. I remembered Lance telling me that it was common to block people's powers, and I wondered if they needed to know what that power was, or if it was a general block. Every little piece of knowledge seemed to come with another ten questions I hadn't considered before. "I'm trying to figure out my powers. Is there some kind of potion for that?"

His smile took all the scary skeleton look away. "There is, but most people try to avoid that option."

"Why?" What I wouldn't do for a fast reveal.

"Well, it's not limited to the witch world. I hear that many normals are drawn to this to find their real selves, whatever that means."

"Like magic mushrooms? I didn't think that was so bad. Not that I've done it. And I guess I heard you shouldn't do it alone, so there's a downside?"

"A mushroom journey is the mildest version of this variety of plant. There are many. Peyote and Salvia are relatively benign, some are habit forming, some are physically challenging, like Ayahuasca, which causes you to vomit for hours. If you wish to attempt a psychedelic, I can only recommend the gentler ones."

"I should probably keep trying research," I said. "I hope Mark finds the killer soon."

22

I had the day off. Well, from work with my part time bosses, anyway. It was a research day for my powers.

Phillip handed me a pile of books he'd pulled from the shelves to help me. The kids' books were still on my nightstand because he wanted me to read them periodically to see if I got any new insights. To be honest, I had to fight my reaction to tell him I wasn't a kid.

My first power was the language thing. Only first because that's the one I knew for sure. The second one? Probably about being able to read people. I didn't know exactly what that meant. Could I tell if they were lying? That would be useful. Or did it go deeper? Like I could tell when someone was lying to themselves? Or had been lied to, or... that was a rabbit hole for another day.

This third one remained a mystery. Without a clue to narrow my research, I'd be reading until I was ninety and still may not know. With a killer to catch, and a business plan to get ready, I didn't have time for another project.

My newly formed gang of snoops agreed we'd spend time tracking suspects. Mine was the husband, and I wasn't sure what my chat had surfaced. Sure, he seemed like a nice, peaceful type. He was definitely carrying a weight of grief, but that didn't mean he was innocent. If it was done without planning, he could regret the murder and grieve his loss. Even though my gut said he wasn't guilty, I still had no proof.

Time to move on, but until we all reported back this evening, I had no direction with the case either. And maybe that was why I couldn't concentrate on anything, and worrying about it just made me feel worse. If I couldn't figure out what to do with all the unknowns, I could test out the one thing I did know — talk to some animals outside the pet shop.

A SHORT WALK from the end of Main Street was a sign for a hiking path. There were bound to be birds, some wild rodents, even a snake. Any of them would help if they knew something.

I stepped through the first trees and found myself on a narrow trail formed by years of people trekking through. I could imagine it closing over if no one passed by for a few days and returning to undergrowth. Another two steps and my ears filled with a buzzing, whispering static. I could hear everything and understand nothing.

I put my hand against the closest tree and used it as an anchor to the world as I closed my eyes and tried to sort out some sense. Nothing came through as words, not like the animals in Lilibeth's care. Did that mean they were speaking English to me? I threw the thought away because it would be easy to answer.

I took a few deep breaths and the volume dropped. Helpful, but not useful. I tried to sort the static into sound groups. The buzzing was different from the whispering, then I told myself to listen only to the whispering in the hope it held words. The buzzing didn't completely go away, but now I only focused on the other sounds. I heard words. "... here... is she safe... I saw her..."

The more words I made out, the easier it became to separate the individual voices. Three creatures were sharing rumors about me. "I would like to talk," I said, feeling like an idiot.

An eagle perched on a branch just above me, the bird's weight bouncing the limb. "Then why don't you?" His voice was high and screechy, and I'd expected a deep and authoritative one. Thank you, all cartoon eagles.

"There's too much noise," I said. "How do I deal with it?"

"How should I know?" The eagle took a step to the side. "Do you think we are like you? No, like every creature, we do not hear the background, only the words directed at us. Your words are too wide and loud. I was ordered to talk and tell you to moderate."

Not very kind, but he'd... she'd... given me good advice. "Thank you. Do I need to preface my words with the type of animal?"

"Not a question I would expect from a witch who hears everything, but I suppose you have not been trained. We know you come from off-island." He looked down his beak at me, and it wasn't just because he was on a branch over my head. "We do not mingle with birds from the mainland. Without magic, there is nothing interesting."

"I'm sure I'll get better eventually," I said, hoping he would see a benefit in answering me. My other power told me he was holding back. I guess it could be about something an eagle would want to keep secret rather than anything to do with me. "I hope I don't offend people in the meantime."

"We are not people," he screamed the words in my head and ears. "Think your questions quietly and towards an individual. For instance, should you need directions from a dog, although I have no idea why you should do so, simply say 'are there any dogs in the area who can answer my question.'"

"Thank you. I guess that will get my mind to think in dog?"

"Yes. Now I must rejoin my family." He spread his wings, preparing to leave.

"Wait, eagle, do you know anything about a dead body?"

"Only that we had no scent of carrion at that place." He gave one flap to his wings and swooped close to my head on his way back to the sky.

23

I remained in the trees thinking long after my snotty informant left. What kind of animal would have witnessed the murder? And how far would my question carry? If I asked, say, a mouse to tell me if anything saw the killing, would it reach as far as the meditation tents?

"Don't listen to everything that birds say." A squirrel clung to the trunk in front of me.

"You understood him... her?" If I couldn't trust what animals told me, then I was lost. Although maybe I should check my assumptions. Why did I think an animal of any kind would be more reliable than any human?

"Oh, him. The hers are much bigger. Yes, he forgot to mention that prey and predator know each other's language. A bit, anyway. I think the eagles and hawks don't listen, so they forgot."

"Any advice? About using my power?" If the squirrel wanted to chat, I was ready to get answers.

"He's right about that. You keep yelling into our heads, we'll start ignoring you, maybe attack. You don't want a cougar getting mad at you. Do humans get into noisy places? I hear outside this island there are way more of them."

I'd attended networking events, and a few clubs where it felt like I was drowning in chatter. In the clubs it was music, and no one was holding philosophical discussions. "We do," I said. "I can use those experiences to figure it out."

"Okay. You asked about that dead she-human. I know her." The squirrel skittered around the trunk to face me. "She put out food for us."

In my experience, people put out food for birds and the squirrels stole it, but life here was so far beyond my experience I had no idea if he was right.

"Do you know what happened to her?"

"No. I don't go up there. This part of the forest belongs to my clan. Dangerous to go far beyond boundaries. I know she was mating with two hes. I liked her house because there was always things to take back to my nest."

So there was a lover? I made a mental note to identify the person, with a caveat that I didn't know if a squirrel was a reliable witness.

"Thank you," I said. "I guess I have to go back to the tents and ask a local. Only squirrels?"

"Only good information from squirrels, yes. If you don't care about good, then there are some raccoons living there, and lots of seagulls. They are liars like all birds. So be careful."

I said goodbye to my little informant and went back to the street. It was only a few steps, but I felt like I was passing from one world to another again.

24

I decided on lunch at the other cafe to explore a little more. Food for Us was situated between the office building and the garden center. Across the way was the little park the community used in fair weather for rites and quiet thought. I'd attend events like that when I had time, but today I hoped to meet a few new people.

"Lunch menu is on the table," the server said.

She was older, maybe fifty. I could see the cook on the other side of the serving hatch. She looked about a hundred years old. It was possible that magic kept people alive and active longer. Or I was a bad judge of age.

I sat at a table at the window to take in the view of the street and park. It wasn't exactly prime people-watching because no one ever seemed to stroll the street, just went into a store and bought what they wanted and then left.

Only two other people were in the café. I didn't recognize either woman. Sandwiches and potato chips on plates and large glasses of water on the table ignored as they stared at me.

"Hi, I'm Cossi Fortuna," I said, trying to be cheerful under their scrutiny. "I'm new here."

The first woman was dressed in a homespun and dyed tunic over loose pants with woven sandals. The outfit looked good on her; someone knew how to sew simple garments to make them look less like sacks. The other woman in jeans and a deep green tee-shirt sipped her water and nodded.

"What can I get you?" The server was back. She wasn't exactly rude but definitely didn't want me here. And she didn't have a name tag for me to use her name. And asking sounded like I was going to make a complaint — at least in my head.

"The tomato soup and a glass of water, please." That was the cheapest thing on the menu.

"Charge to your account?"

"Yes," I said. "I'm sorry, I don't know your name."

"Wendy." She turned away and called something into the kitchen that sounded like 'guess water and Adam's ale'.

"Don't worry about her," the homespun woman said. "She's like that with everyone. Like taking the time for a kind word would cost her something. I'm Violet Bark. I live in the earth witch village. This is Effie Walsh, runs the grocery."

"Nice to meet you," I said. "I'm still trying to find my bearings, and my powers."

"Never heard of anyone your age still searching," Effie said. "Your dad didn't give you the exercises?"

"My dad didn't tell me anything about magic," I said. "So far, anything I know about this world is what people have told me. I know I have three powers, but the only one I'm sure of is language. I might be able to read people, but the third one escapes me."

"You'll get there," Violet said. "Sometimes the knowledge is buried deep, and you need to believe in your own abilities to access them. Language is easy to identify. Can you speak to all witches?"

"Do witches speak in different languages?" Was I operating on the assumption we all spoke English?

"We have a few French speakers, and one German, but mostly here we're English." Effie rolled her eyes at Violet. "She doesn't always get it right. Did you mean in their heads, Vi?"

Violet laughed at herself. "Of course. I was thinking about telepathy. Do you mean actual language?"

Wendy deposited my soup and water; there were two packages of saltines on a side plate. It seemed very old fashioned but somehow comforting. Then she went away without a word.

"Yes. I can understand whatever language someone is speaking. Including animals. Some of it is in my head, some of it seems to be just like talking. I'm not sure I can speak anything but English."

"Useful," Violet said. "Perhaps you can come to my place and talk the slugs into eating elsewhere?"

"Happy to give it a try." It did sound interesting, and I might be desperate enough to have a purpose here that I'd be the local slug whisperer. "Any advice on how I would confirm my other power?"

"There are a lot of flavors of reading people," Effie said. "Can you tell when someone is lying?"

"Yes. I've always been good at that," I said.

"Can you tell if they are planning to lie to you?" Wendy asked from her seat at the counter.

"I've never tested it."

"Am I planning to lie to you?" Wendy asked.

I closed my eyes and focused on her. "Yes. But it's not a big lie."

She grinned. "Yeah, I was going to say I liked your hair, but I don't. You should get it cut short."

"Leave her alone," the crone in the kitchen called. "You're jealous of her curls."

I sipped my soup, and it was like every perfect tomato in the world was sitting on my tongue. "This is marvelous."

"Zoe is the best kitchen witch on the island when it comes to comfort food," Wendy said.

"Jan does good work with the new stuff, but some of us like basic grub," Violet said.

The bell over the door rang and I looked to see Mrs. Vestum walk through the door and then take a table in the corner. The warmth slipped out of the room.

25

She looked at me over her menu. I tried to ignore it, but the conversation with Effie and Violet had died. Wendy stood waiting for Mrs. Vestum's order with no sign of impatience. Was everyone afraid of her? Did she wield some power over everyone? She was my nemesis on the council, and I needed friends. That's why I started talking to the two women. I mean, I liked them right away, but I did have an agenda.

"BLT and lemonade," Mrs. Vestum said.

"So the usual?" Wendy said. "Coming right up."

The menu had been a cover for her staring evil at me. I'd faced bullies before. I went to school after all.

"Lovely day," I said to her like we were friendly.

"Why are you here and not at that other place? Where you get a meal for free? The council support isn't unending," she said.

"Her lunch is on the house," the cook said. "Welcome gift."

Mrs. Vestum just hummed a response.

I wasn't going to leave it at that. People were being kind

and she was using that to make them feel bad. "I thought I should take in more of the town," I said. "Get to know people. You know, settle in, find a way to contribute."

"You mean manipulate people into giving you what you want?" Mrs. Vestum cast a glance at the table where Violet and Effie were paying their bill.

"It was nice to meet you two," I said. "I'll take you up on that offer, Violet. How do I reach you?"

Violet smiled and stared at Mrs. Vestum as she said, "Just head over to the earth witch village. During the day, anyone will point you in my direction."

Wendy placed the woman's order on her table and walked back to her perch on one of the counter stools. She didn't make eye contact with me or the old woman.

"I was trying to learn about my powers," I said to Mrs. Vestum. "It's a big adjustment finding out I'm a witch."

"That excuse won't work much longer," the woman said before taking a bite of her sandwich.

"I'm working on it," I said. The only way to get around her distaste for me was to keep treating her like I didn't notice it. The tactic had worked many times in the past. My reading people power wasn't getting past her veneer of general anger at the world. The annoyance at me was only a small part of her mood. "I'm also working on supporting myself. I'll bring a business plan to the council soon." I wasn't going to arm her with any details to derail me.

"So you thought you'd make friends with the weakest council members?"

That was mean, but she did think they were weak. I couldn't tell if it was just because they didn't like her, or if they were weak in magic. "They seemed very nice. Violet is going to help me find my other power. I like people, so it's not a surprise I can make friends."

Mrs. Vestum took a long drink of her lemonade. Movement in the kitchen caught my attention. Zoe was leaning on the serving hatch, watching us. Wendy was pretending to add up her receipts, but she couldn't hide her interest in the conversation from me.

"Friends won't approve a poor idea," Mrs. Vestum said. "You are expected to do the work. On your business plan and on your powers. You are struggling with something a five-year-old knows."

"Too bad I wasn't on the island as a child."

As soon as the words were out, I knew I'd made a mistake. Zoe stepped back and Wendy moved away to start cleaning tables. It was the equivalent of the saloon clearing when the gunfighters stood up. There was nothing I could do to take it back or defend it.

"If your mother was a better witch, you would have. I do hope you didn't inherit her recklessness. Or your father's blind devotion to an idiot."

All the angry responses ran through my mind. I managed to keep them there and not make it worse by blaming people for making them leave. I didn't know enough about the circumstances to defend my mother right. You could bet when I did, I'd do whatever it took to clear her name.

Wendy was staring at me wide-eyed, her mouth forming the word 'no'.

I pushed my soup bowl to the center of the table and stood. "Thank you, Zoe, for the lunch. It was delicious. And Wendy, you were kind to offer me a chance to test my power. I have work to do, so I'll leave you for now. Mrs. Vestum, good day."

26

I spent the rest of the day preparing my business proposal for the council. I'd been playing around with the concept too long, pretending I couldn't get anything done until the crime was solved. Not true. It was the perfect time to research and document my ideas. The proposal didn't need to be a complete plan, just enough to get approval to go to the next step.

Lilibeth picked me up at seven and we rode out to the Howling Place to meet Lance and D for an update on the investigation.

Lance put pints of cider in front of us and sat in the final chair. We were sitting at a corner table. Not that it would keep our conversations private from shifter ears, but to indicate privacy. Sheena said that people would not listen in unless we made our voices so loud they couldn't be ignored.

"Tell me what you think of this," Lance said. "New crop, and I added some elderberries to the process. I'm not sure it makes it through the apple flavor."

I sniffed the aroma, and he was right; apples predominately and just a hint of earthy sweetness. Taking a sip, I felt the bubbles dance on my tongue like champagne. "Ooh, it's subtle but there. Kind of like blackberry and wild blueberry?"

"You like it?" he asked. "Sometimes we make a flavor that doesn't resonate with the normals. I like that you come at it with that perspective."

"I more than like it." I rarely drank cider because it always tasted like apple core to me. I was definitely on the road to this being my favorite drink.

"I'll send a batch to a friend to see if it travels well. Okay, we should start talking about what we found, right?"

I pulled out a notebook. "I'll keep track of all the bits and send you an update." I told them what I'd learned from the squirrel. "If you told me two weeks ago that I would be taking a statement from a rodent, I would have laughed nervously and run away."

"Welcome to our world," Lilibeth said. "I got a bit from Mark. He asked me to keep an eye on you, Cossi. I think he might like you."

"Or I'm his number one suspect." Mark was hot in that bad boy turned cop way, but I didn't have time for any entanglements right now. "What did he say?"

"Mrs. Macy didn't die from a fall. Someone bashed her head in. And, maybe this is more helpful, the spell from the rue and daffodil was cast before she died."

"So she might have cast it on herself?" D asked. "For something she did? Then she met the killer. Whatever it was, do you think they did it together and she was going to confess? That's why she had to die?"

"What about this lover?" I asked. "Anyone know who it might be?"

"I guess that's a priority," Lance said. "I didn't smell anyone on her other than the flowers."

"Would the flowers cover up other scents?" I asked.

"I would have caught a hint. So either they weren't together lately, or... I don't know. If the flowers were there before she was killed, then other scents should have been on top."

Lilibeth took the notebook from me. "Okay, so we have a list of suspects. Mr. Macy. I agree he's the closest to her, so logically a suspect. We have this mystery lover, that's not enough. Who else?"

D opened his notes. "I looked at her activity in the last few days. Where her phone was, what she spent money on. Mrs. Macy didn't leave the island. She texted three people, her husband, her supplier, and a burner phone in Sechelt. I can dig deeper."

"I'll add the person with a burner phone to the list," Lilibeth said. "You think someone else was on the mainland, getting her supplies?"

"A burner?" D shook his head. "Unless someone lost their phone and had to buy an emergency one. But how would she know the number?"

Lilibeth added the questions to the notebook. "Did anyone have an argument with her?"

"Mrs. Vestum," D said. "I heard them arguing the day before we found her. I told Mark, but I don't know if he followed up."

"Anyone want to take her on?" Lilibeth asked.

"She'll report me to Dolph," Lance said. "He's the alpha, Cossi. I have enough problems with him as it is."

"She hates me," I said.

"She hates everyone," D said. "I'll take her on. She's always having technical problems. Maybe one of you can come with me?" He looked at me like I hadn't just said the woman couldn't stand me.

"If you think I can help," I said, resigned to doing things I didn't want to for the case. "Sure. Just let me know."

"There's one person we should add," Lance said. "I can't think of a motive, but Phillip was on the mainland when that call was made."

"Picking me up," I said.

"He's still a suspect," Lilibeth said, "but not high on the list. And if we have to investigate him, we'll leave you out of it. At least until you are able to move out."

"So," D said, "I think we have our orders. We all need to be on the lookout for the lover. Mr. Macy needs to be interviewed, or whatever we're doing to suspects."

"I can do that," I said. "I'm interested in potions and medicinal teas, so I have a reason to talk to him." And since I was the only one who seemed to think the jealous husband could be the killer, I was the only one who would ask the right questions.

27

I worked in the bookshop the next morning. My schedule was going to keep me busy until the afternoon, so I planned on dropping in on Sweet and Bitter then. Working with Phillip gave me a chance to do two things. One was getting his ideas on my proposal. Since he was a council member, I figured it would give me the right perspective. And I could try to settle my feelings about him being on our suspect list.

He was on the ladder shelving books a customer had returned. The store was part retail and part library. Most of the business seemed to come from borrowing; only a few books were bought, and mostly by off-island communities.

I was sorting cards to see if anyone was hoarding books. Not illegal but frowned on.

"I wrote my proposal last night," I said. "Would you look it over? I mean, it's a first draft, so I've probably left things out or there's different requirements than on the mainland."

I refiled the cards and then started with the pile of new books. Well, new to us. Everything needed to be sorted and categorized when it came in or it would be chaos in a few hours.

"If you like," he said. "I can't help too much because it would be a conflict of interest. Lilibeth or Jan can give you better advice though. It hasn't been long since they put their own business ideas through the process."

"Does everyone have to go through it?" I asked.

"A few businesses have been here so long that there were very few rules when they started. As the non-magical society became more complex, we adopted some of their systems. I inherited this store from my parents, so I only needed to prove I could keep the level of quality high. Some of the farms simply pass from generation to generation with nothing more than a nod of acceptance."

I got that the island needed to have paperwork in place for all the rules outside. I'm not sure how they would deal with an audit, but that wasn't my worry right now. "I ate at Food for Us yesterday. Great food, and Zoe seemed like she'd been around for a long time."

"She's the original owner. At first, the island's inhabitants didn't need restaurants or bookstores, or a potion shop for that matter. Then more people came, then the earth witches split to their own village, then the shifters asked to set up here. Things got complicated and busy. Having someone cook for you is sometimes the difference between eating and just plowing through research or experimentation until you pass out." He laughed as if that was a funny quirk of the island.

"Students are the same way," I said. "That's why universities and colleges have fast food places that deliver. So, how long has Zoe been the cook?"

"I'd have to look up the exact date, but about a hundred years."

"No way!"

"Witchcraft gives you a longer life. Unless an accident takes you, most of us live for a couple of centuries, no slow decline. Just a few days of weakness to indicate you need to say your goodbyes and then we stop."

"And if you leave the community?" My mom died in a car accident, but my dad got sick.

"You lose the... I suppose it's an ambient protection? And if, like your father, you don't continue a solid practice, your human side becomes dominant. We are all human in some way, even the shifters."

"Thanks. There are so many things I don't know that I can't even think of what questions to ask. I'll go get my proposal." I ran up the stairs so Phillip wouldn't see my tears. I guess I'd shoved my grief aside because of all the shocks of my new world. Maybe I could be my first customer at the meditation center.

My phone rang as I dried my eyes and took control of my emotions.

"I have some news," D said.

"Good morning, great to hear from you."

"Yeah, yeah. Lance heard a rumor that Dolph was messing around with a witch. It's not uncommon, but maybe he's the lover? Or if not, he'll know something to point us in the right direction."

"We can go there this afternoon. I'll talk to Mr. Macy tomorrow."

"The shifter village is off limits. Dolph called a Howling. Only shifters allowed. It's starting now, and the earliest we'll get in is the day after tomorrow."

"Okay, then I can go when it's clear."

"Lilibeth will do it," D said. "I wasn't asking you to go. I was giving you information. The day after, the shifters will be worn out and have a few injuries. She goes in and does a bit of first aid. Energy potions, bandages, a few pain-damping herbs."

"So it will be more natural for her to ask questions," I said. I really wanted to solve the crime myself, but we'd formed a team for a reason. "I'll talk to Mr. Macy today. What about Mrs. Vestum?"

"I've left a message asking if I can come check on her devices. I'll let you know."

We said goodbye and I went back to work with my proposal for Phillip's feedback.

28

Phillip's advice was to talk to the island accountant and lawyer before finalizing my proposal. He called and they were both in the office, so he gave me time off to ask their advice. Or, as I liked to think of the paperwork involved in both situations, get it over with.

The lawyer was waiting for me outside the business center. Dick Moses looked to be in his mid-forties, but given what Phillip told me, could have been eighty. He also looked like he'd be more comfortable hanging ten off the coast on a surfboard.

"Ashley is just finishing up with a client," he said with a warm smile. "Let's have a look at what you're planning."

I'm sure he meant the business, but I couldn't help thinking about the case. If he was the only lawyer on the island, he'd defend the killer. And prosecute? Another completely alien thing to figure out.

He led me to a small office on the first floor. No name on the door, just a black number 3 in beautiful calligraphy. Inside was a desk, two chairs in front and one behind it. A cellphone and a laptop sat on the top.

"Where are all the law books?" I blurted it out because I'd lost control of, or used up, my ability to pretend nothing surprised me here.

He gave me another warm smile and gestured for me to sit. "All online. I keep some files at home, but we all use these offices when we need to. You might think of booking one so you have a quiet place to work."

I sat as he indicated, and he took the chair across the desk. "Okay, so you want to use the land by the tents to set up some kind of retreat?"

"Yes, meditation and perhaps a place for someone to focus on their powers, or... if it was on the mainland, I'd probably say a place to recharge, but I don't know if that's appropriate here."

"It is. Not so much for the island residents, but plenty of the mainland communities have no safe place to focus on research or simply relax. You do know you can only market to witches?"

"Yes, I guess there's some kind of list, or coded phrases, or a witch web, where I can market. That's something I can investigate later. I don't want to waste your time, so what are the legal issues?"

"The land is owned by the council, so you'll need to apply for a lease," he said. "Give me your email, and I'll send you all the forms. And the usual business registration. I'll do it for you, so we don't have anything slip about our home."

"I'm happy to get all the help you have to offer. Are you really the only lawyer here? What happens if people sue each other?" I was careful not to ask specifically about the murder.

"Mediation. We don't have a court system. We also have very few conflicts that aren't sorted out by the parties involved."

"And criminal matters?"

"Ah, you think we have prosecutors and judges. No. The Crown doesn't have jurisdiction. We play along with some rules because it keeps nosy inspectors off our backs. Anything that requires punishment comes before the council. We assign what normals would likely call Restorative Justice. People make amends for their mistakes."

Not an option given to my parents. I still didn't understand how they were going to get the killer to atone for Mrs. Macy's death, but I couldn't think of any other questions that would get me more than a 'let Mark deal with it' answer.

"That's great. Thanks for sending the forms. I should probably see Ashley before I head back to work."

"Lovely to meet you," he said and stood to shake my hand. "Ashley will meet you on the second floor, door seven."

Ashley met me in the hall instead. She was about ten years older than me and looked like a model for a goth girl. Dark, straight black hair, pale skin that somehow glowed. If she was wearing a layer of eyeliner and a black lace dress, instead of a forest green business suit and no makeup — all the goths in Vancouver would have been worshiping at her feet.

"Did you get what you needed from Dick?" she asked, not inviting me in.

"I did, thanks," I said. "He told me you'd let me know the accounting side."

"Right now, you don't need to do anything. We have a central accounting system that produces every report and filing you need when your business is up and running. When you have your approval and registration numbers, send them along to me and I'll schedule a training session."

"That sounds perfect." I knew from my projects how easy it was to go down rabbit holes of administration when you didn't have the basics in place. "I guess thinking of a name might help sell the project to the council."

"Yes." She turned and locked the door behind me. "I don't have any more time. My uncle is having a hard go of it. His wife was murdered, and the investigation seems stalled."

29

I knew if I went back to the apartment, I'd start working on the forms for my business. I was pretty much burned out with that subject for today.

It would be helpful if I didn't have to deal with so many critical tasks. Settling into a completely unexpected new life, getting a business off the ground to avoid a massive debt, and solving a murder might be more than I could handle. But I already had friends, and people helping me with the business and the murder, so I was making progress.

As much as I was desperate to discover my powers, that had to be on the back burner for the moment. I mean, it did act as a conversation starter, but people were going to wonder about my ability to retain information since they all gave me the same answer.

So, it was time to talk to Mr. Macy again. Now that I knew the relationship between him and Ashley, it occurred to me that I had one more item to add to the to-do list. How had I missed the relationships? With such a small population, family connections must be complex. How did they manage to keep from marrying their first cousins?

Sweet and Bitter was empty when I walked through the door. No Mr. Macy, no Ashley, no customers. I'd hoped Ashley wouldn't be here because I didn't see her on the street after we talked. She'd gone out a back door and I had gone out the front. The center and the store were on opposite sides of the street, so I figured I would have seen her cross.

I stood at the counter and looked for a bell or something to get attention. There was a door behind the counter that must lead to an office, or storeroom. No bell, no note to say he'd be back in a minute.

"Mr. Macy?" I called out.

"In a second," he answered.

The last time I was here, we'd talked about 'shrooms, among other things. I wasn't willing to give up control to find my power, yet, but it might be a service I could offer at the meditation center. Oh, and add 'get a name for the business' to my list of tasks. At least I didn't need to come up with something cutesy like in some of the paranormal books I'd read.

Mr. Macy walked out of the back room, followed by Mark. At least he was out doing some investigating.

"Cossi," Mark said in acknowledgment of my presence.

"Mark," I responded in a matching tone.

He turned to Mr. Macy and said, "I'll update you when I have more information." He nodded to both of us and then left.

"Is there progress on the investigation?" I asked.

"Mark has shared a few pieces with me. I can't tell you anything. Henbane is not an easy place to keep secrets, and Mark asked me not to share."

"Fair enough," I said, as I tried to come up with a way to bring the topic up again without seeming suspicious. "I guess the killer shouldn't get a progress report."

"Exactly," he said. "What can I do for you today?"

"I just talked to your niece," I said. "She's helping me with my business proposal. The process is a little different here."

"Yes, Ashley took over from her mother, Deirdra, who is out traveling the world, probably won't come back until she needs to say her goodbyes. I'm glad she's helping you. She's taken me on as a project, as if I can't deal with my grief without her help."

"Grief is weird," I said. "I was so angry at my dad when I found out what he'd been hiding from me, I didn't get to the crying stage." My throat tightened as I said the words.

"You will," he said. "If you don't soon, come see me. I have a potion to help you see your inner feelings. Get past the angry to the deeper emotions."

"I will. When I'm not so busy. Speaking of which, the other day, when I came by, you said you could lead some spiritual journeys, 'shrooms and stuff."

He reached for an appointment book. "We can arrange a session if you like."

"Oh, not for me. I wondered if that would be a good service to offer at the retreat. I guess two questions. Do you think there'd be a market, and would you be interested in leading something like that?"

He tilted his head in thought. I could just read his feelings through the blur of grief. He wanted to, but right now he couldn't see that far into the future. He needed to heal. If Mark had given him an update, he was unlikely to be a suspect. That is, if Mark gave him real information rather than using it as an interrogation technique.

"I think it's a brilliant idea," he said. "We are fortunate to live so deep in nature. Many communities are in cities where they don't get peace for anything, and they are burdened with keeping normals ignorant of their powers."

I didn't want to push him too hard about leading sessions. "What would I call it so other witches know what they're getting?"

"It's a seeking," he said. "I'll think about leading it, and if I can't, then I can recommend someone."

It dawned on me, or my powers read it in his mind; I was asking him to come to the place his wife's body was found. "That would be perfect," I said. "I'm sorry, I didn't think about how hard it would be for you to go up there."

"I will heal past that feeling. It's nice that you were able to read my sadness."

"It will be easier when the case is solved," I said. "Too many questions and not enough answers right now."

"Mark is waiting for some test results," he said. "Perhaps in a few days we can all move past this terrible event."

30

I worked at the cafe for a couple of hours to give Jan some time with his new side hustle. He put together a weekly menu and recipe list with the spices and herbs all included, and a grocery shopping list. He'd asked me about how normal people grocery shopped so he could make something for the non-magical people. Since pre-prepped meals were all the rage, I thought it was a good idea. And since he wasn't including the protein or produce, he could send it all to the mainland.

"So what do you do with the money?" I asked. The island wasn't about how rich you were, just how you supported yourself. Without a profit motive, I couldn't understand why Jan had this hustle, as well as the cider one with Lance.

"I like to take a vacation every year, so some of it goes to funding my travels, and I do need supplies from the main-land. But most of everyone's profit goes to the island. Pays for all kinds of things, the school, the medical center, the cost of higher education."

The entire island ran like a co-op? "Then I'll be contributing when my business is up and running. I like it."

"First, you'll pay back what you owe. All the costs of setting up your place come from the pool. When that's paid back, you contribute what you can." He handed me a list of groceries. "Can you see if that will work?"

There were no patrons, allowing me to sit at a stool so I could still chat. "This will work for a family or four," I said. "No problem getting the ingredients in a grocery store. For two or one person, they'll have lots of leftovers. If I remember the market research right, this kind of thing is most popular with single people."

"It sounds like I need a field trip," he said. "Interested in coming and showing me around a grocery store?"

I'd seen some small stores on my way in, but checking them out wouldn't help. They would be more likely to offer smaller portions because they knew their clients better than a large chain store.

"On-line. I'm not saying I'd turn down a trip to the mainland, but you can see what's on offer by going to the larger store websites."

He came out of the kitchen and put his laptop on the counter. "Show me. I think I can easily create a single meal version with a 'use up the leftovers' dish at the end."

We spent an hour testing out various options of ordering produce before he had enough information, and we cleared the cart.

"It's quiet today. You could just put up the closed sign," I said. "We haven't had one customer."

"But then you wouldn't be here to help me," he said.

That was kind and made me glad I'd been useful.

"I asked Mr. Macy if he'd be interested in doing some of the activities at the meditation center," I said. "What about catering? Would you deliver food to us? Or I could pick it up?"

"Where do you expect people to stay?" he asked. "And how many at once?"

It was good to talk business with someone and push away all the worrying about my powers and the murder. Maybe Mark would solve it before I had time to get back to my investigation.

"There's room for a kind of hostel layout. Small rooms for up to three people. A central gathering place for socializing. The tents will have the option of a cot. Until I get going, I don't want to get into better lodging, too much expenditure and potential delay without knowing if I can make it profitable. So, three people to twelve at the most. If I get to capacity."

"Okay, we can work something out," he said. "Zoe and I can put a proposal together for you. We could offer a dinner once a week where one of us comes on site?"

"Perfect," I said. "I'll think about other ways for the people on the island to get involved. I've been thinking about a name for the place."

"If you keep calling it the meditation center, then that's what everyone will call it."

"I know. So, I thought maybe The Inner Spell."

"It does tie to your idea of meditation and research," he said. "It sounds like you're planning more than just a 'making the space available' kind of thing."

"Well, a business plan tends to expand the scope," I said. "I think I need a mix. Programs I run, and simply space to think and do your own thing."

"You know, when the murder is solved, we'll do a cleansing. We should do it at the tents. Not just because it's where the body was found, but also to free the land from the death."

"Where would it happen otherwise?" I thought a cleansing would be done at the place most affected. And I hadn't even considered the fact that my clients on the mainland might know about the murder.

"The park," he said. "It's more about helping the entire island move past the pain. You'd probably have a smaller ceremony before you start making changes, but if we all gathered there, it could be more potent."

"I guess Mark will solve the case soon," I said. "Long before I start working on The Inner Spell, assuming I get approval."

"Mark thinks he'll have the answer when he gets the test results back," Jan said. "I don't know if he's right to be confident. Spells can change things, making tests useless or worse, misdirect him."

We'd get the answer regardless. I didn't care if Mark solved it before me if the killer was found.

The door opened and a woman walked through looking around as if trying to find someone in a crowd. Since the cafe was empty, she didn't take long.

"Are you Cossi Fortuna?" the woman asked. I nodded and she continued. "Violet mentioned you were seeking knowledge. I'm Lily Valley. Your presence is required at the earth witch chamber."

Jan closed his laptop and stood. "You should go now," he said.

31

I wasn't sure whether Jan was afraid of the earth witches, or he just wanted me to get it over with, but I followed Lily back to the bike park and then along past the future site of The Inner Spell to what looked like dense forest. Only a short distance past the first of the trees I saw a hut to the left, and the outline of roofs ahead. It seemed like the whole island was like that. Transitions from one reality to another through trees.

"You can leave your bike here," Lily said as she dismounted and leaned hers against the trunk of a giant Douglas fir.

"Is there anything I need to know first?" I asked, following her example. The earth witch chamber appeared to be the hut. It was round with one door currently sitting open and a thatch style roof. I couldn't see inside because it was black.

"Just be honest," Lily said. "No one will hurt you."

Some kind of test? "I don't know much about anything," I said. The last thing I wanted was to disappear inside that hut and never be heard from again. Jan knew where I was, but would he try to find me if I didn't come back?

"You were asking about your powers," Lily said. "This is one way to find out. Maybe it will work, maybe not. Are you saying you don't want to try?"

I reminded myself I was on a magical island, not in Vancouver. Here, I'm sure different rules applied. On the mainland, I'd never agree to go into a dark space with a stranger no matter what promises were made. Here, magic was normal, and I had been trying to dig up that third power. And it's possible I'd get some other answers. And Phillip would notice if I didn't come back, and D and Lilibeth. One of them would report me missing to Mark.

I took a deep breath and said, "Let's go."

"When you step inside, close your eyes. I'll have my hand on your back to keep you steady."

"Why? I mean, it's dark. I won't be able to see anything."

"Do you question everything?"

"No... yes. Things I don't know, like being told to walk into a dark hut and close my eyes."

She gave me an impatient nod of her head. "I suppose I can understand that. Fine. Once we're inside, the door will close and then we'll take the hoods off the lanterns. It can be hard on your eyes to go from dark to bright light. But do as you wish."

I stepped inside far enough to let Lily through and then closed my eyes tight. I heard the door scrape on the earth as it closed, and then felt her hand on my back. It was grounding in the absence of any other point of reference. I could hear breathing but had no clue how many people were inside. A faint scent of rosemary and charred wood came through.

"Blink your eyes open but keep your gaze on the ground until your pupils adjust." This was a man.

I did as he told me and was glad of the order, or possibly advice delivered in a commanding tone, as three LED camping lanterns shone bright white light into the tiny space.

When I felt like I could take it, I looked up. Lily stood to my right, Violet to my left. The other earth witch was the man. Tall and dressed in jeans and a denim shirt, his gray hair hung in straggly curls to his elbows. He smiled and I felt safe.

"Welcome," he said. "You know Lily and Violet. My name is Alder Bark. Violet and I are hand-fasted. We brought you here today for a seeking because you have not been properly trained."

I ignored what I heard as a jab at my parents. He probably didn't mean it that way, just a statement of fact. "Only really my third power seems elusive," I said. "I can read people and understand any language, including animals."

"All useful skills. And we have no language witches at this time, so useful and welcome."

"What does this seeking entail?"

"We drink tea, and I seek through your mind with questions. My power allows me to find the truth that may be hidden even to yourself."

"What kind of tea? I can't just go on a trip," I said. "I have things to do."

"Simply relaxing herbs," Violet said. "We all drink from the same pot. You can go last, so you are assured it is mild and safe."

I was here, and they were promising me information I wanted. I just hoped I wouldn't get information I didn't want. The truth isn't always helpful.

"Okay."

Alder turned and picked up a tray holding a teapot and four mugs. Violet held the tray while he poured. She passed it to me with instructions to take a mug and pass it to the left.

When we were all standing with mugs in our hands, Lily downed hers, then Alder, then Violet. I looked at the liquid and sniffed like I could tell what was there. I had no clue, but I did feel the intentions around me. No one was plotting my demise. I tossed the contents down in one gulp just as everyone else had done.

32

A warm sense of comfort blossomed from my stomach. No matter what happened, I would be safe. I heard a tiny paranoid voice in my head saying I was taking a huge risk, but the feeling of wellbeing shut it up.

"I will begin by asking you to think back to your earlier days," Alder said, "for any memory of being different." He took my hands gently in his. "This contact will allow me to follow your thoughts. If you feel any discomfort, please speak up."

I nodded, not willing to speak and break the spell. I pictured my school, kindergarten. The gerbil in the corner told me it was thirsty. The teacher didn't believe me and said I had a very active imagination.

"Come forward, what is the next memory?"

It was a bit cloudy, I guessed it was the tea smoothing out the anxiety I felt when I didn't really fit in. Just teenage stuff, really, and Mom and Dad said everyone felt that way. I knew differently.

"Another."

In business school. A memory of a group project and knowing one of the participants had no intention of doing the work. Then a stabbing pain made me gasp and pull my hand out of his grasp.

"I'm sorry," Alder said. "The pain will fade now that we are separate."

He was right. As soon as our hands let go, the pain vanished.

"So? Did you find anything?"

"The kindergarten memory was the first time you spoke to an animal?"

"I guess. I mean, I don't remember anything before that. I didn't remember it happening until right now. And my parents agreed with the teacher. Just my imagination."

"Your first power manifested at the usual time," Violet said. "Around five or six years old. Your parents protected you, and I'm sure they thought it would fade if you didn't use it."

"In your teens, you were much older than most children here in manifesting your second power. You knew your peers felt different to you because you could read their inner feelings," Alder said.

"And the third one?" The tea was wearing off and irritation replaced comfort. My parents kept me from being a witch. They should have told me.

"The pain," Alder said. "Someone placed a block on your powers. I imagine it was done between the first and second incidents. It is odd that there is such a long period between your chat with the gerbil and the last time you recognized your power."

"There was a blank spot," I said. "I have no idea what happened, or even when."

"It means there was another incident. I think the block

needed strengthening as you got older," Violet said. "It happens sometimes."

"When you decided to return to us, the protection started to fade," Lily said, patting my hand in comfort. "This last one is stronger. Perhaps something that needed intense training to control."

"Can you tell who did this to me?" Maybe it wasn't my parents. If we could get enough information, we could identify the person who did it and get them to reverse it.

"The thing about this kind of spell, Cossi, it's only done as the powers rise. Each power has a different spell," Violet said. "Did your parents change your diet at any time, or give you something unusual to drink?"

"Yes. Dad was always making me drink his potions. So, it was him?"

"Most likely," Lily said. "Although he may have had help. I hope not from here. Your parents were trying to protect you. You don't need it now that you are here with us."

"If witches are safe here, how do you know about these blocking spells?" There was some ugly secret here on Henbane that I was about to learn.

"We need to use them," Alder said. "Very rarely, a power rises that only causes harm. Witches cannot choose to ignore their powers for long. We have had the occasional thief power rise, for instance. The witch must be in agreement when we offer a power block."

"How did my dad make it work? I never agreed that he could cast a spell on me. Or could another spell make me forget? Or is there a loophole?"

"No, it's not that. The spell will work even if it's administered secretly, as yours was. It is a law. Anyone found forcing a power block will be subject to a block on all their own powers, and exile from their community. They may still live on the island, but as outcasts."

I had so many questions I was about to burst. "So eventually my third power will unlock. And if it's destructive or something, I just ask for a block?"

"Yes, but you can't know your power is like that," Violet said. "Even the most beneficial power would be a danger to you living among normals."

"And has anyone refused a block lately?"

"No," Alder said. "Are you thinking about Leanne Macy's killing?"

"Yes, aren't you?"

"There is no power to make a witch kill someone," Lily said. "We should let you go back before it gets dark."

There could be a power that gives someone motive to kill. I kept the words to myself because it was clear I was being dismissed.

33

I was still shaken about what I'd learned when we met to update our progress on the case. So much so that I wouldn't talk about the ceremony to my friends. I needed to process — a phrase I never thought I'd say. I normally just ran head on into a problem until it was solved. Of course, sometimes things got worse at first, but that wasn't my fault. People should listen to me sooner.

"I'll be at the village tomorrow most of the day," Lilibeth said at our meeting. We were in D's home to avoid being overheard by any of our suspects. "Dolph contacted me, and it was a big howling, so lots of scrapes, bruises, and epic hangovers."

I was still trying to get used to the way the islanders managed things like medical help and policing. "Just you? It seems like a lot to take on."

"I'll call Doc Rene if I run into something I can't handle. We all heal pretty well from minor stuff. The shifters like to get back to normal as soon as they can, but without me, they'd rest up a day or two and that's all they need."

D was typing on his keyboard. He'd set up a spreadsheet

to keep everything we knew in once place, and we all had access. It didn't mean we would check it, but it would come in handy when we got close.

"Cossi," D said, "what's your update? It's easier on me if we all go around rather than just talk."

"Okay, I talked to Mr. Macy. I don't think it was him. I know I need to understand how my powers work, but he didn't give me any lying vibes. He's sad but not angry. He's looking forward to the future. I think he's pushed all his grief aside until Mark finds the killer."

I thought about the other events while D typed. "I've heard about Mark's tests a few times. No one seems to be very confident."

"Who?" Lance asked. "It might be important to know how the news is spreading. I mean, no one thought it would be kept secret; that rarely happens on Henbane. But if Mark is telling people about the tests, maybe he's looking for reactions."

I doubted that anyone would spontaneously confess over a lab test. "Do you have everyone's DNA on file?"

"Not that kind of test," D said. "He sent it to a research community. I'll give you a contact there at some point. It's just the kind of group that will want your services. Looking for traces of powers. I think Mark is hoping to identify the killer through the magic they use."

"There are overlaps, right?" I said. "And anyone can learn a spell?"

"We're getting off track," D said. "Yes, there are overlaps, but not many for all three powers. And anyone can learn a spell, but unless you have the right kind of magic, the results will be weak. What else did you learn?"

"That powers can be blocked. Would that have anything to do with the murder?"

"I don't know whose power was blocked," Lance said. "For sure no shifter. Dolph wouldn't allow anyone to change their natures. Shifting is complicated, and things can go bad if the balance isn't right."

"My cousin was blocked," Lilibeth said. "Remember? He stole from everyone when he was a kid."

"Yeah, but they lifted it when he learned control," D said. "Blocking is mostly for serious punishment these days. Like the killer will be blocked and exiled depending on why they murdered Mrs. Macy."

"Did my parents get blocked before they were sent away?" I couldn't help it. I needed to know more about the people who'd protected me by taking away my power rather than telling me what I was and teaching me.

D looked at Lilibeth like he was hoping she would answer. I would not use my power to read my friends because it felt like a huge betrayal. So I was guessing at his motive.

"Your parents fled, Cossi," Lance said. "Nobody likes to talk about it, but we shifters don't like secrets. A spell went wrong, really wrong. Your parents grabbed you and a few things from their home and took one of the boats to the mainland before anyone came looking."

"What would have happened to them if Mom and Dad had stayed?" It seems like today is going to be one of those days that just keeps hitting you in the gut. I wanted answers, but I'd kind of thought of my parents as the good guys in the scenario.

"Some punishment," D said. "Maybe blocking for a while. Mistakes happen in magic. Your mom was experimenting when the council told her to leave it alone. I think everyone was just pissed at her for being so stubborn."

I blinked back the tears I could feel pushing behind my

eyes. If they hadn't run, my mom and dad would be alive today. And I'd know everything about this witch world. No wonder Dad said not to come here in his letter.

"What else do we know?" I said, desperate for a subject change.

"Rumors," Lilibeth said. "That her lover was an earth witch. I still don't think it matters, but you wanted to find him."

"I believe you," I said, "but we need to know who it is so we can eliminate them. I mean, Phillip is on the list, do we think he's the killer?"

Lilibeth held up her hands in surrender. "I'm not arguing, but I don't know where to go from here."

"A squirrel said I should go talk to the animals up at the tents," I said, remembering I hadn't updated them on my most recent forest chat.

"When are you planning to go?" D asked. "We need to see Mrs. Vestum tomorrow."

"Are we set up for that? I can go this afternoon to the tents."

"Yes. Tomorrow at one. I'll come get you so you don't get lost."

34

I felt like an idiot. I'd ridden up to the tents to talk with squirrels and raccoons, and basically any animal that would cooperate. I'd learned that just because I could talk to them, didn't mean they always wanted to talk to me. Just like humans.

There was a circle of sawn-off logs that formed seats just to the left of the cluster of tents. The circle was large enough to have a fire pit in the center, a brick affair that had been cleaned of ashes. I guess even the island wasn't safe from the wildfires we experienced every year.

I took a deep breath that tasted of pine and dust, then tried to calm myself. It didn't work that well, as every time I thought I was there, the idea of talking to squirrels and raccoons about something as important as a murder made me giggle. I hoped one day soon it wouldn't feel so ridiculous.

There weren't any animals in sight right now. It was still pretty early and if I had to guess, this was nap time. I probably need to do some research on the habits of the creatures first, but this was my first time slot available, and I'd rather be here than talking to Mrs. Vestum.

I grabbed a handful of the seed and nut mix Lilibeth handed me before I cycled up here and strewed it in front of me. "I'd like to talk," I said. It wasn't quite a shout, but I wanted my voice to carry.

While I waited, I took in the whole space where I wanted to build my future. There was plenty of room to put a little cottage if I decided to live up here. I'd be one of the solitary witches if I chose that option. The idea didn't feel like it was right. I wanted an apartment over a store, or an existing little house. Since there wasn't a big movement of people coming and going from Henbane, I imagine there were no empty houses. Maybe someone like Ashley's mom, who was off exploring, would rent me their place.

"Are you going to talk?"

The voice startled me out of my dreams. A squirrel sat in front of me, nibbling on a peanut. "Yes. I came up to ask if anyone saw what happened with the woman."

"The killed one. She was dead already. We didn't stay to watch because the he carried the dead she inside. Not our business, and dangerous. We don't spy."

Disappointing. "Would any of the other animals know more?"

"We know a lot, but it was just us out here. The raccoons were off stealing food. No one else saw."

My second power didn't reach the animal world. Being able to read the emotional state of people wasn't helpful so far, and I had some clue as to what a human should feel. How could I expect to read the thoughts and motivations of non-humans? Whatever it was, this was a dead end, and I didn't have time to waste.

"I guess we'll have to look elsewhere for clues," I said. "Thank you for your time."

"Why are people coming here now? People only pass by for many summers. Now they drop their dead here. They say a few words and sprinkle smells."

"I don't know why the killer came here," I said. "Maybe because the place is mostly deserted. When we catch them, I want to start a business here. That's why I came up to look at the tents."

"You will bring more people?"

"Not too many. I hope they won't disturb you." What was I going to say? I was sure if I needed the animal's permission to use the place, someone would have told me by now.

"Will they bring food?"

"I can make sure we provide supplies," I said. "I didn't think you would be running short since there's so many plants around."

"Free food is better." The squirrel twitched his tail. "Nest stuff is good. Maybe protection is good."

He kept listing items, so I just talked over him. "Is all that stuff for you or for all the animals?"

"Me. Some of the other squirrel families. Not raccoons, not birds."

"We can come to an agreement that suits everyone when I get approval," I said. I wasn't going to become the supply witch for this area, but I could make an effort to help out. "I'll come back when we find the killer."

"The he was sad," my friend said.

"Can you tell me what he looked like?"

"Yes. A he witch."

So helpful. "If she was dead when he carried her in, how would I find out where she was killed?"

"Blood. Ask a death eater." He darted down on all fours

and scanned the area. He'd managed to eat all the food I'd spread out. "All gone. Bye."

No other animal answered my call, and I was out of bribes. Did I have to go looking for some kind of vulture? Or, had Mark found the kill site? Was that what he'd sent out for testing?

35

Phillip was standing outside the door to Raziel's books when I got back. "The council is ready to see you," he said. "Get your proposal and tidy up a bit. I'll take you in."

I had no time to update anyone on what I'd found. I was the only one who knew it was a witch and that somewhere on the island a bloody mess was waiting to be found.

I ran up to the apartment and looked in the mirror. Great. My hair looked like I'd put it in a blender and added twigs. Curls don't respond well to brushing, so I clipped them in a bun and smeared some aloe gel on my face to deal with the sunburn.

Everything about the business was in my laptop, but none of it was printed. If I took the time to make paper packages for each council member, nine of them if my memory served, I might do more damage to my reputation. And they wouldn't have time to read anything before I could convince them of the value I saw in opening a business to bring people to the island.

Laptop under my arm, I rejoined Phillip on the street. "Is it far?"

"The meeting room is in the office center," he said. "Come on, this won't take long."

He was excited about this meeting. I had at least one ally on the council. I'd need more than that to counter Mrs. Vestum's general hatred of me. But one was better than none.

The room was set up like a town hall meeting. Eight people sat at a long table at the front, and three chairs faced them in the middle of the room. I felt exactly like I was going to be interrogated. If they were going for intimidation, they'd aced it. The only saving grace was D sitting at the far right of the table. I had no idea he was a council member. Or any idea how to feel about not knowing.

Mrs. Vestum was sitting in the center, and when Phillip left me to join the others, she knocked on the table with an actual gavel. "Settle down. It's time to start with this newcomer."

Silence. I just stood there with my laptop under my arm, wondering if I needed permission to sit, and where I was going to set up.

"Sit, girl," Mrs. Vestum snapped. "We don't have all day. I suppose I should introduce you to the members. Then you get ten minutes."

I took the middle seat, leaving one on each side of me if I needed a totally useless table.

"You know some of us. Didier Rothtect. He's here to cast his father's vote. You know Phillip Raziel and Peter Macy, I've seen you in his store. To my right is Dolph Amarok, the shifter Alpha."

She paused like I didn't need to know the other names. I smiled and nodded, and then waited for her to continue.

She huffed a little displeasure and then continued. "You met Violet Bark and Effie Walsh in the cafe, so I don't need to elaborate on their roles. And I believe you met with Ashley Ivers. The final member is Jeffery Peak. He represents the solitaries who prefer to live their lives separate from the other communities, but do not wish to leave the care of the island in our hands alone."

"Pleased to meet you," I said.

"I wasn't finished. You must learn manners." Mrs. Vestum glanced at Philip and then turned back to me. "Mr. Raziel has recused himself from voting. He will minute the meeting. Mr. Peak will exercise his role as tie breaker if needed. Now you may elaborate on the information you provided."

I didn't remember providing anything but before I could put my foot in it again, D spoke up. "I forwarded your final proposal for the council to review." He gave me a look that reinforced what I was getting from my power. Don't mention the investigation. And that made me realize I couldn't read anyone else. Some shield thing? Or just too many people and not enough focus?

"Thank you for that, D." I put my laptop on the chair while I tried to think what she expected me to elaborate on. "Are there any specific questions?"

Mr. Peak cleared his throat. He wore black, all black, jeans, shirt, and the jacket slung across the back of his chair. His hair needed a cut, and his beard was braided. He'd gotten the style from someone, or online. So, not a complete hermit.

"What about the impact of your clients on the island culture?" he asked in a voice that seemed creaky with disuse.

"I will do a thorough impact analysis in the next stage," I

said. I had no idea that would be needed, but it wasn't difficult to ask a few people about their fears. "My business will only bring a few people to the island, and the services are set up to keep them to the area near the tents."

"And you will transport them to and from the island?" Dolph asked. "Witches only, is that right?"

He stared at me while he asked like he could smell my nervousness. As a werewolf, he probably could.

"At first, but I am happy to talk about other options."

He sat back in his chair and folded his arms.

No one else had any questions and I didn't have a clue what to add to whatever version D sent around. I guess I'd relied on my power for so long I didn't notice how hard it was to figure people out if you couldn't read them.

"It's time to cast our votes," Mrs. Vestum said with a little smile on her face.

They went down the line. D voted against me. "Sorry, Cossi, it's my dad's vote so I don't have a choice."

By the time we got to Mr. Peak, the vote was four in my favor and three against. He stood and looked at me before casting his vote. "Your idea has merit, Ms. Fortuna, but I think you need to focus more on your business plan than whatever else is taking your time. I vote no for the solitaries, making it a tie. I break the tie with a vote of 'not yet'. You must do more to convince us that your enterprise will not endanger the concealment of our home." He put his jacket on and left.

Mrs. Vestum's smile was gone. She'd hoped to get a clear 'no'. "Apprise us of the next date when you think you are ready."

36

D tried to talk to me, but I wasn't ready. I'd been ambushed, and I know he wasn't at fault, but I was too mad to separate him from the rest of the people who'd just wasted my time.

"Let me know when we can talk to Mrs. Vestum about the murder," I said. "I guess I need to go home and think of a way to get all the answers the council might decide they need."

"I'm sorry you didn't get notice about the meeting," he said. "You were up at the site and your phone must have been off."

"I just need to be alone for a bit," I said. "See you tomorrow."

I didn't wait for him to say any more. I went up to my room and shut the door. Phillip wasn't home yet, so I could have grabbed dinner, but I wanted to avoid being interrupted while I got my thoughts straight.

I made notes to set a survey up to find out what everyone was afraid of if I got approval. And what they saw as benefits, because some people were happy I was trying something new.

The activity gave me something to do with all the anger. By the time I finished making notes and strategies, I was ready to figure out why I was feeling guilty. Mad, I understood. Disappointed, sure. I knew it often took a few tries to get people to see the value of something new. Betrayal? Well, that was just stupid and probably more about anger and disappointment feeding off each other.

Guilt?

Why?

The little dig from Mr. Peak about focusing on my business hurt. He didn't know me, and how I could do more than one thing at a time. Maybe if I left the murder case to Mark, I would have thought to survey the residents. I'm pretty sure Mrs. Vestum would have found another reason to get everyone to say no. She was determined to make my life miserable.

It wasn't about the council, not completely. I'd found out my parents lied to me all my life. I know Dad said something in his letter about that, but now I knew how little I could trust my memories of being a kid. And I didn't have anyone here I could talk to about it. Why was that?

Because my parents pulled me away from my life and made me a stranger to the people I should think of as family.

Running through the problem over and over wasn't helping. Every revelation just ramped up my anger. I closed my laptop and then sat on the floor, legs crossed, hands on my knees. If I couldn't get through this with logic, it's possible emptying my mind would break the cycle.

It took so much longer than usual to release the busy

thoughts in my mind, but I got there. And I stayed there until I heard voices in the house. Phillip was home, and he had a guest. They spoke quietly and I couldn't hear the words, but the sound disturbed my peace. Luckily, I'd banished most of the emotions. I still held onto a bit of annoyance at Mrs. Vestum for setting me up. And myself for letting it happen. But I could think now.

I let the ideas about my business percolate in the back of my mind while I worked on the murder. I updated the conversation I had with the squirrel into the spreadsheet. I still wasn't ready to talk to anyone, but they could read the information now.

I wondered who to ask if there were any vultures around. I could talk to one about the murder site. Or think of a way to get Mark to tell me. But trying to figure out the identity of the killer was like bashing my head against an invisible brick wall. I needed a different approach.

If I didn't know the people on the island well enough to guess if they were capable of murder, I did know that they were people. Motives were the same no matter if you were a witch, shifter, or normal, right?

Money, love, anger or fear, revenge. That pretty much summed up my knowledge of motives. Money wouldn't work here, and I couldn't think of a substitute. Love? No matter how many times my friends told me taking a lover was normal, I didn't think they were right. In my mind, anger and fear were basically the same. Was there someone on the island afraid of Mrs. Macy? Something she knew? Something she saw?

Revenge didn't ring right. Sure, there seemed to be petty stuff going on, Mrs. Vestum's entire life as an example. But I didn't sense anything stronger than irritation around me.

This wasn't making progress; in fact, it was showing me

how little I knew about everything in life. I did have something to talk about when the four of us got back together to update our investigation. I'd take that as progress. And I had actions steps for my proposal that would work for cover when I wanted to interrogate someone.

37

When I pictured turning a discussion about my business into a hunt for clues, I didn't anticipate the first opportunity being Mrs. Vestum. Having to talk to her the morning after she'd so gleefully turned down my proposal made everything worse.

"She's like that with everyone," D said as we walked to her cabin. "She's been mad at the world as long as I've known her."

"There's something personal when it comes to me. Maybe my parents did something to her, or she thinks I should pay for my mom's mistake. Or she hates redheads."

"Or it's just that she had more opportunity with you. No one else is looking for her approval."

That could be it. But she wasn't the only nay vote. "Why did your dad vote no?" Was Mrs. V controlling the votes?

"He told me he had too many questions. I know we gave you some advice, Cossi, but I don't think any of us knew how different your thinking is from ours. I promise we didn't sabotage you. You can trust us."

That was sweet. I hadn't even thought any of my friends

would purposefully undermine me, and not just because my power would have shown me, but because they were friends. "I should have thought more about the culture. I know it's different here, but with the investigation and my jobs, and everything I run into every day about magic, I dropped the ball."

"We'll try harder," D said. "Like today. I told Mrs. Vestum you were coming because your knowledge of the normal world might help me see what the problem is. You can ask her all sorts of questions if she thinks you're doing her a favor. Just be gentle so she is less likely to get her back up."

"What is the problem?" If I had to pretend expertise I didn't have, I needed more information.

"There isn't one. Every now and then I throttle her bandwidth." He grinned at his evil plans.

"You are terrible, D. I hope I never get on your bad side."

"I doubt you'll ever do anything to annoy me," he said.

We arrived at her door. It was a basic house, not an evil witch one. Clapboard sides painted a deep green, red door and trim. Like every other house I'd seen, it fit into its surroundings like it grew there.

"You're late," she said when she opened the door. "Let's get this over with."

"Good morning Mrs. Vestum," D said. "Happy to help out."

"It's your job, Didier."

She barely acknowledged me as she stood aside to let us in. The interior of the house was neat and clean. A desktop computer sat on a desk tucked into a corner, a small sofa and two comfy chairs made up a conversation area around the fire. The coffee table, which sat in the middle of the furniture, was a slab of oak on a stone base.

"It doesn't respond to my commands," she said, pointing

at the computer. "I have communications to send to colleagues in other communities. If I don't respond in a timely manner, they will never let me forget it. Do what you think is needed."

I pictured her in a chat room with other miserable witches sharing stories about how they made people cry.

"It's a common problem," I said. "Did you get any warnings? Like notices that pop up on your screen?"

"You would do better focusing on your business instead of poking into every distraction that comes along."

So she thought I wasn't taking the Inner Spell seriously? "I'm going to talk to people about what they think of the idea," I said. "You were right to turn me down. I need to get to know the island better so I'm more aware when I'm making assumptions."

"It sounds like you're planning to waste as much time as possible," she said.

I worked with people like her in school. No way to satisfy them or ignore them. The weird thing was I didn't read anything in her that was nasty. The overall feeling I got from her was protective. So D was partially right. It probably wasn't personal. Not that it made me like her, but I could work with someone who was protecting... her home? Her way of life? Did it matter?

"In the end, it pays to take the time you need," I said. "I want to contribute to the community, not change it. I'm hoping to get approval next time I come before council."

I looked over at D. He was on his knees, feeling behind the tower. If he said the problem was a loose wire, I would give the whole plot away by laughing.

"Pretty words. I'm not swayed, young lady. Your actions tell us more about who you are than what you say. See that you don't get in the way of other witches in your search for information."

"I'll be careful," I said. "I'd like to get your advice before I go further with the survey. Perhaps you know who I should meet first, or what questions I should ask." If she got involved, maybe she'd be less determined to stop me.

She squinted at me and pursed her lips. On the face of it, she looked completely skeptical, inside she was pleased, more than that, flattered. Yay me!

"So, you will stop interfering with Mark's investigation?"

I was premature with the congratulations. She still wasn't as angry and bitter as she wanted people to think, but I'd take any progress in our relationship. "I'm not interfering. I want the killer caught like everyone else. Mr. Macy needs to know the truth, don't you think? And selfishly, I want the land to be free for me to develop."

"There are secrets here that are best left between the people who have lived on Henbane for their entire long lives."

She was done with helping me. "D, did you check the cache?" I asked. "I seem to remember that can slow things down a lot."

He turned from the screen and grinned at us. "Just finishing up. You'll be back online in five minutes."

38

I must be getting used to Mrs. Vestum because I walked away with no anger or even irritation at her behavior. I kind of felt sorry for her, but not enough to like her. I guess there was a reason she was so mean to everyone, and when I got time, I'd dig into her story.

"What did we learn?" D asked.

"You mean other than she can't tell when you are lying to her?"

"Yeah. Her powers are all about protection and connection. I mean, she's great at getting to the details of something, like your proposal, but she doesn't know when to stop picking. That's why we have a council. So no one person holds power over our lives."

That was interesting, and it shed some light on why she took so badly to me. My mother was a threat to the island, then I came back and boom, there's a murder.

"She'll feel better when we find the killer," I said. "The island will be safe again, and we can all move ahead."

He nudged my shoulder with his. "Oh, life is never simple here. Yes, we haven't had a murder before — or maybe only at the beginning and no one remembers. Find the murderer, and some people won't believe you have the right person. Or that they deserve punishment. Or that you should be punished for making trouble. We're people, Cossi. We have powers that make us hard to understand. Mrs. Vestum, for all her meanness, can read connections like no one else."

"Maybe she should be investigating." Seeing the connections could mean she knows who was involved in the murder. "Or is Mark using her?"

"I doubt it," D said. "Who would answer her questions?"

"One thing she said right at the end intrigued me. That there are secrets here that everyone keeps. Is no one willing to talk because they're afraid of where it will lead?"

"Then Mark isn't going to solve the case," D said. "I'll leave you here. Lots to catch up on since I added investigating criminals to my to-do list."

I waved goodbye and decided to take a longer route home. Through the forest where I could think. Or talk to a few furry inhabitants. We weren't making progress, partly because we were all too busy to really investigate. Mark kept his work close so no one would gossip about what they knew.

The trees closed over me again after a few steps. Insects buzzed in the background, maybe talking or just working. Wings cast a shadow over me, then swept away. I found a clear space at the foot of a large sequoia and leaned against the trunk. It was time to question my priorities. This seemed as good a place as any.

I had to be honest with myself and recognize I was scattered and trying to do too many things at the same time. My business proposal had been lacking because I was trying to figure out my powers and solve a crime. Learning that my powers had been blocked was a huge step, but I couldn't imagine how I could do anything about it but wait for the spell to dissipate. That could take years. I was making no headway on the investigation because I was too worried about my business and curious about my powers.

One thing at a time. It was the only way to make progress.

My business plan was important, but I had time. My powers were on hold until something changed. The investigation was critical, but Mark was on the job, and I had no real reason to go behind his back to solve it. And I had no skills beyond what I'd learned on TV.

"Okay, Cossi, let's get organized. One more day of real investigation and if you don't find anything, you leave it alone." I'd see if my friends could spend a day with me but if not, I was going to talk to Dolph and anyone else I could think of to get answers. Then my business proposal was my only priority.

"Do you have any food?" My squirrel friend was sitting at my side.

"Not today," I said. "I talked to your cousin. I think so, anyway. I talked to a squirrel up at the tents."

"Yes. He sent a message. You gave him food."

"I'll make sure I bring some next time," I promised. "He said I should talk to some carrion eaters. They can help me find the place where Mrs. Macy was killed."

"Dangerous," he said.

"Probably, but what else can I do?"

"Small ones. Marmots. Not birds, they lie. If you want to talk to one, go in day. Do not tell them you talked to me. Go to dogman village. Edges. Goodbye."

He scurried up the tree and disappeared.

At least I didn't need to try to get the attention of a vulture or eagle. Tomorrow I'd start at the shifter village.

I stretched out my arms and stood. I had a shift at Run, Fly, Slither in an hour. Time to take a shower and change.

The apartment was empty when I arrived. I grabbed a muffin and a glass of water before I jumped into the shower. Ten minutes later I returned to the kitchen to see what I might find to carry for bribing small animals to talk. There was a note on the table. Folded handmade paper with my name on the front. Not Cossi, but my full name. And not in Phillip's handwriting.

Keep your nose out of things that don't affect you, or I'll make sure they do.

39

The note gave me chills. I'd never received a threat before. Ever. This must be from the killer. It was time to go back to Mark. This was no ambiguous feeling about the murder. Someone was worried enough to stop me, and I had no idea what magical consequences could be, but just the creepy feeling I was the next body should be enough to scare me off. Except that wasn't the emotion that rose first. Determination to get this person locked away sprang into my head. I don't know if that is an emotion, but that's what I felt.

For a second, I thought my first stop should be D, or Lilibeth. Not just to let them know about the note, but to figure out who sent it. Lance was over at The Howling Place, but my other two friends were in the village, only a few minutes' walk.

But only for a second.

This wasn't doing a side investigation. If I didn't hand this over to Mark, I'd be withholding evidence. Even if the island worked on different rules, I didn't want to actually get in Mark's way; I just wanted the crime solved.

I sent him a text. The number was in a directory like the olden times. Phillip kept his copy in the kitchen. *I've been threatened. Note in the kitchen. All doors were locked.*

Enough detail to get his attention, but not all of it. I didn't want to carry on a text conversation about notes and locked doors or anything about the case.

Where are you?

Phillip's kitchen

On my way.

I put the kettle on and then returned to the note still sitting on the table. I'd only touched it enough to open the fold, so it was possible I hadn't disturbed evidence. I took a picture of it and sent it to all three friends, letting them know Mark was on his way.

Three similar answers came back. *We need to catch this witch tomorrow.*

Mark knocked on the back door before I could respond with a date and time to meet.

"Where is it?" he asked. No hello. No how are you feeling? All business, which should have reassured me, but it just got under my skin. I'd been threatened because he hadn't done his job. I didn't give voice to my thoughts. I'm not completely clueless.

Roy padded in behind him and sat at my feet.

"It's on the table," I said.

"You smell of fear," Roy said.

At least someone cared. "I'm trying hard not to be too scared."

"Did you do anything but touch it?" Mark asked as Roy and I joined him.

"No, what kind of things would I do?"

"I guess you haven't had spell training, so nothing." He took his own picture and then pulled a bag of fine yellow powder from his pocket and sprinkled some on the note. My fingerprints darkened the paper. No other prints but a few places where the powder turned a shade deeper.

"Gloves, or a cleansing spell," he said to himself. He used a pair of tweezers to shake the yellow off then added a sprinkling of magenta powder. "No particular magic signature, but definitely a spell."

He repeated the process on the back of the paper with the same results.

"What about the handwriting?" I asked.

"I don't recognize it." He looked at Roy and then me. "Let's try something new." He picked up the note with the tweezers again. "Tell Cossi if you know who wrote it."

"Wait. How do you usually work together? I'm happy to translate, but he's your partner."

"We work together fine, Cossi. Your contribution is valuable, now you're here, but we were fine before you even knew about Henbane." Mark held the note closer to Roy's nose.

Roy sniffed near the paper and backed up to sneeze.

"Witch magic, not shifter. Male, but there's pepper in the ink so I can't get a real scent."

I passed the information on. "Does it help?"

"Knowing it's a male is better than nothing." He put the note in an evidence bag and placed it back on the table. "You sure the doors were locked?" It came across as an accusation. Like I was too naive to lock my doors.

I thought I'd told him about the killer being a man. Maybe he'd forgotten or hadn't listened. Or I hadn't given him the update. In cop mode, he wasn't the kind of guy I wanted to spend any time with, let alone date. Of course, I'd only seen him on the job, so maybe he was different socially.

"Unless Phillip came home and then left them unlocked, yes. I had to use my key to get in."

"There are spells to open doors." He led Roy to the back door. Roy sniffed at the lock and the floor.

"Nothing but you and the man who lives here."

I passed on Roy's analysis. "The other door comes from the store. I think Phillip would notice if someone snuck up here."

"I need to check anyway. Thoroughness is important."

Roy didn't get close to the door before sneezing.

"I guess they came through the store," Mark said. "Someone Phillip would trust."

"Am I safe?" This wasn't getting us anywhere. And despite my belief in Phillip as my mentor, he'd moved up my suspect list. It could be he'd been fooled into leaving me the note, but he could easily be the author, and put the pepper around to confuse the investigation.

"You should probably avoid being alone," Mark said. "Better to have a couple of people around at all times."

"What about here? It's often just me. And someone finds it easy to get in and out."

He reached into his pocket again. They were normal-sized but seemed to contain as much as a backpack. He retrieved three small green cloth bags, two tied with a blue ribbon and one with red. "One for each door. Put the blue ones on the outside doors, the spell will let in anyone who lives here, or anyone escorted by you or Phillip. The red one goes on your door, no one but you can pass."

I took the bags and thanked him. "Do you think you'll have the killer soon?"

"I have some solid leads," he said. "You'll know when everyone knows."

Roy had no comment.

40

I met with Lance, D, and Lilibeth the next morning in Lilibeth's apartment because I didn't fully trust the security measures Mark gave me. He'd updated Phillip on the note and the protection bags. Phillip had asked if I wanted him to arrange another home for me. I said no because unless I moved in with Mark, there was no other place safe enough. Mark was sexy in a walled off emotion way, but I wasn't getting under his control.

Staying didn't mean I could ignore the threat. I'd jammed a chair under the handle of my bedroom door. I kept jerking awake throughout the night. Too much of this and I would lose my hold on reality.

"Mark didn't find anything on the note?" Lilibeth asked for the third time. "Could he have pretended?"

"I would have known. Whoever left this was an expert at hiding his identity. We only know it's a he because of my chats with Roy and the squirrels." I still expected everyone to snigger at the idea I could get reliable information from a rodent.

"So, Mrs. Vestum is firmly off the list," Lance said. "I

didn't think she'd have the strength to move a body anyway, but it's nice to have confirmation."

"Are we adding anyone else to the list?" D asked. "We need to work out our plan for the day rather than just running around."

"What about Dolph?" I asked.

Lilibeth put up her hand like we were in class. "I talked to him while I did the post-howling damage control. He isn't our guy. He only tolerates the witches. He would never take one as a lover. And there's no other motive."

"How long ago did the shifters arrive?" I asked. If he was the first alpha, it would be weird for him to resent the people who gave him a place to live. Okay, I know some people resent everything, even kindness.

"About fifty years after the witches settled," Lance said. "Dolph is the tenth alpha."

There was some emotion behind his words I couldn't quite label. When I had time, maybe I could dig into it and help him. I was making a long list of 'when I get time' tasks.

"He doesn't represent the feelings of the pack," Lance continued. "And I'm not sure if it's just misplaced resentment. He got everything he wanted, so he should be happy."

Definitely a story there.

"Mr. Macy was my assignment. I'm willing to say he's not our guy. He just seems too calm and balanced to build up enough emotion to kill."

"Phillip?" D asked. "He was at the bottom of the list before. Now he's our only suspect."

"I don't sense any threat," I said. "And he was picking me up around the time Mrs. Macy died."

"So just this secret lover?" Lilibeth said.

"What about Mark?" I asked. "If he's the killer, he has all the opportunities to hide his actions. He could have left the note for me and then pretended he didn't find anything on it."

"He can't," D said. "First of all, there's no spell strong enough to block his lies from you. And his powers are all protective, and his oath of office is binding. Magically binding."

"Okay, we need to find the actual murder site, and anything to lead us to the killer's identity, right?" I hoped someone would come up with another lead, but I guess narrowing it down to these two actions from a list of people we didn't think were killers was progress.

"Shifter village first," Lance said. "Dolph is off-island, so we should be okay to hang around without him chasing us off."

"And we can have lunch at Sheena's." I hoped the kill site would give us everything and we could take the final clues to Mark for an arrest.

41

The ride to the entrance of the shifter village took long enough for me to think about the questions I'd put to a marmot. Okay, based on my lack of knowledge of marmots, and my slight knowledge of squirrels, I felt not quite completely unprepared.

"There's a den over there," Lance said, pointing to a break in the trees. "The small animals don't like us. Shifters, that is. I'm not sure why because we've never hunted them."

That left me, Lilibeth, and D to step into the shadows.

"Look for a rock pile, they shelter underneath," Lance called after us.

"Do you have to get close to their home?" Lilibeth asked. "If there are young, we'll have trouble."

"I want to get to their territory," I said. "Making them come to us seems a bit demanding."

We found a clearing just a few paces in. In the middle, two large blocks of rock formed a triangular arch. Small tracks ran in and out of the space.

"I'd like to speak to a marmot," I said to get attention of

the creatures. I turned to my companions and said, "You two just wait behind me. I've never done this with an audience."

D and Lilibeth moved to the edge of the clearing. As soon as I was alone, a shiny nose poked up from the debris under the arch. The body that followed looked like a giant guinea pig. I stood still and let him or her come to me.

"You are that new witch?"

"Yes. How did you know?" Was there some kind of animal gossip site?

"Heard a new witch came. You ask a lot of questions, too. And you want to know about dead places."

Well, that cut short the plan I had to convince the marmot to talk to me. "Yes. A witch was killed, but we don't know where it happened. A squirrel told me to ask around here."

"Squirrels have no brains. It's good you came to us. Yes. A witch died not near here. The dogmen would know the scent. On the other side, where the other witches live. Near the other water."

"How do you know about it?" If the shifters would have smelled the blood, did that mean the killer knew exactly where to hide the scent?

"Other dens. We talk."

"Do you know anything else about the location?" I didn't look forward to searching the whole western side of the island.

"Big trees, sharp rocks, noisy water." The marmot scurried a little closer. "Food? Heard you pay in food."

I pulled out a handful of seeds and nuts, then put them on the ground. "Thank you."

"So?" Lilibeth said. "That was weird to watch, and we barely heard your side of it."

"This is an island full of witches and shifters, and me

talking to an animal is weird?" I laughed. "Let's get back to the road so I only have to repeat it once."

A HALF HOUR later we were standing on a rock that jutted out over the water. A stream washed into the sea just to the side of our perch. The cove below was narrow, and waves crashed constantly on the cliff face.

"Noisy water," D said. "Sharp rocks, and these are the oldest trees on the island."

"And there's blood," Lance said, sniffing in the direction of the densest trees.

"Can you lead us there?" Lilibeth asked.

"Just stick behind me," Lance said.

We walked from our rock toward what initially looked like a solid wall of trees. When we got closer, I could see it was only three huge trunks. Lance led us through the gap and then around two more giants. All the time I could hear the waves trying to bash the island apart.

"Through there," Lance said, pointing at a final space between two even larger trunks. "Should we tell Mark?"

"Let's look first," I said. "No point in wasting his time if there's nothing there."

"There is," Lance said.

I went first. As I approached the entrance, the warm, clean smell of the forest changed to something darker.

The ground was dirt and a scattering of stones. The trees didn't allow for enough light to support undergrowth beyond the debris around their roots. A flat rock like an altar was in the center of the clearing. Flies swarmed around the dark stain on the rock.

"I guess we know something happened here," D said. He held up his phone and turned in a circle. "I don't have a signal, but it's time to get Mark out here." He left to find enough bars to call Mark to our location.

"While we wait," I said, "we should see if we can find a clue. Otherwise Mark will shut us out again."

"I can't go down there," Lilibeth said.

"We shouldn't disturb the scene any more than it has been. I think we'll be okay just checking around the edge," I said.

Lance nodded and moved to patrol clockwise while Lilibeth and I went the other way. I wasn't sure how long I would be able to take the smell, but I was determined to get something that would catch the killer and make me feel safe after the threatening note.

Lance joined us after only a few minutes. "You go way slower than me in wolf," he said.

Lilibeth bent down and picked up something from the ground. "Cossi, this is something."

She held a clump of tangled gray hair.

"I found this just before we met," Lance said. He opened his hand and there was a silver earring in his palm.

"Earth witch for sure," Lilibeth said. "We have to give these to Mark."

42

D returned while we were talking about our finds. We all had experience gained from watching TV crime shows, but none of us were confident that the lessons would apply in the normal world, let alone on Henbane.

"We could put them back where we got them," Lance said. "That way Mark can see them as we did."

I didn't want to let go of any evidence, even for a few minutes. "We could put a marker where we picked them up," I said. "That way we don't risk losing them. I'd hate to have to explain how we lost important evidence."

"Mark will be here in a few minutes," D said. "I'm with Cossi. We've already touched these things, so Mark knows we found them." He reached into his pocket and showed us the contents in his palm. A coin, a length of string, and a plastic card like a credit card but blank.

Lilibeth took the card and placed it carefully at the site of the gray hair and Lance spun away to put the coin in place of the earring. "Don't do anything interesting until I get back."

"What can we get?" I asked. "Does anyone recognize the earring?"

"The earth witches tend to use silver a lot," D said, "and the symbols are really common." He took a picture of the objects.

Lilibeth held the hair out. "Lance might get someone's scent."

"Is there an earth witch anywhere near our suspect list?"

"Mark's only a few minutes away," Lance said as he stepped around the closest tree trunk. "Let me get close to the hair. It's just a small sample, and it's been contaminated with the odors of the clearing and forest. It's a long shot, but I can try to tell who the scent belongs to."

He directed Lilibeth to hold the strands in her fingertips and let them hang down. He leaned in and sniffed. Shook his head and took one more inhale.

"Well?" I was afraid of Mark stomping into sight and demanding we stop.

"Male. The daffodil and rue are there, so the oils were applied here or before they arrived. There's pepper and garlic. They are hiding the finer scents. Sorry."

"Better than before," I said. "We've got the murder site now. Why would Mrs. Macy come this far into the forest? Is there something here that doesn't grow anywhere else? It doesn't strike me as a good place for a tryst."

Lance glanced over my shoulder. "He's here."

I didn't even hear footsteps. "Okay, we start talking about this as soon as we're released. Maybe an earth witch noticed someone missing an earring."

"Good work," Mark said as he appeared. "I told you to stay away from the investigation, but finding this is a big step."

Not exactly a thank you, but I'd take it. "We found some

clues," I said, pointing to the hair and earring. "There might be more."

"Stay here," Mark said. "I need to walk the perimeter. Where did you find these?"

"The hair was over here," Lilibeth pointed to the plastic card. "There's a coin where Lance found the jewelry."

"I won't be long." He walked to his right and started to move around the edge of the clearing.

"Can we talk, or will he hear us?" I asked.

"Just keep it quiet," Lance said. "I can hear him moving, so he can't surprise us."

"We need to tell him our suspicions," D said. "It's looking more and more like Cossi's right about Mrs. Macy's lover being the killer. I'm not convinced, and we don't have a motive, but no one else is on the list."

"You said that having a lover was not a problem," I said.

"Not a cultural problem," Lilibeth said. "Personal one? But wouldn't that put Mr. Macy on the top of the list?"

"He's not the killer," I said. "I can read people, remember? I didn't get anything off him but sorrow."

"Whether it's the lover or her husband, we don't have the motive," Lance said. "We have to tell Mark what we think."

"But he'll tell us to stop investigating," Lilibeth said.

"And when has that stopped us?" I asked. "If we'd listened the first time he warned us off, he wouldn't know where she was killed."

"He's almost back," Lance whispered. "Before he gets here, I think there's a spell blocking me from identifying and tracking this guy. Maybe a couple of shifters together could break through. You want me to come back tonight with someone?"

"You missed a couple of things," Mark said. "I'll take the clues you found and send them for analysis."

"For DNA?" I asked. "Or something else."

"You need to let me do my job," he said. "All of you. It's dangerous for amateurs to get in the way of a killer. And Cossi, you've already been threatened."

"We're all fine, no attacks, no evil spells. And we have some ideas," I said, giving up on getting an answer about the tests.

"What?" Mark pulled out his phone. "I'll record it."

The others looked at me. "Fine, if I forget anything, jump in."

"One at a time," Mark said. "Or you'll make it impossible to use the recording for proof."

"I don't know what you already found out," I said, hoping he'd fill in some blanks, but he just nodded at me to continue. I told him our theory about the lover and pointed out the obvious link to the earth witches. I told him about the discussions with the squirrels and marmot. "So you probably want to start interviewing the earth witches."

"I'll add your information to the file, but even if Cossi doesn't know, the other three of you are perfectly aware that we don't just go interrogating people without a lot more reason. Now, I've told you more than once to leave this to me. If you don't listen this time, I'll have to arrest you and let the council figure out the repercussions."

He ushered us back out to the road where our bikes waited. "You need to leave first," he said.

"Dinner at the Howling Place," Lance said. "Drinks on me."

43

I wasn't sure how the day got ahead of us. I was glad to be out of that clearing before full dark, thank goodness for summer days with late sunsets.

The ride to Sheena's bar was long enough for me to process what happened. Mark's warnings to stay away had ramped up. He'd never hinted he'd lock us up before.

I couldn't think, bike, and read the feelings of my companions at the same time so I was saved from violating my own rule about using my power on friends.

The bar was half full when we arrived. It was still a bit early for a real dinner, but I wasn't the only one starving. Lance left us at the table to go to the bar, saying he'd take care of ordering. Normally that would get my back up, but now, I let him do his thing. He knew the menu and the drinks, and by now he knew my preferences, along with those of D and Lilibeth.

He returned with beer and glasses of water. "Dinner will be up soon. We can talk here."

I drank the water first, not wanting to slake my thirst with beer on an empty stomach. The aromas from the kitchen were an appetizing mix of grilled meat and roasting vegetables.

"That'll wash away the taste from the clearing," D said, nudging my beer toward me.

I took a sip, and the taste of molasses and lemon flooded my mouth. I hadn't realized how much of the experience clung to me until the flavors cleaned my spirit. "Okay. So how mad was Mark?"

"I was going to ask you that," Lilibeth said.

"My powers were dulled, now that I think of it," I said. "And Mark was... blocked? No, that's not the right word. His emotions were filtered. Is that possible?"

"There's a spell for everything," D said. "I'm guessing no one really wants their hidden self read, so you'll start noticing people take steps to protect themselves."

Great. I had a useful power and a semi-useful one and a tightly locked up one. "So I will only be able to talk to animals soon?"

They laughed and clinked their mugs.

D took pity on me. "We were wondering when you'd figure out that we're not all walking around with our magic hanging out. Most of us keep charms on us to ward off the more intrusive powers. Witches can't stop using them, so it's important to have a defense."

Our talk was interrupted by a shifter girl with long blond hair and green eyes delivering our dinners. Chicken kebabs with roasted vegetables and bread. "Enjoy." She winked at Lance and bounced away. Lance's gaze followed her until she pushed through the kitchen door.

"So do I have some kind of protection? Am I leaking out information I don't know about?" If I was, it would explain Mrs. Vestum's response to me. I didn't like her, and she knew exactly how much.

"Did Phillip give you anything when you met?" Lilibeth asked.

"No, but my mother gave me this before she died." I held out my wrist to show the bracelet she'd insisted I always wear. The anger I felt at the way my parents lied to me rose up, like mentioning either of them pulled a trigger. I ignored it, hoping it would sink back down into the recesses of my subconscious.

"That's protection," Lance said. "It must have been hers when she lived on Henbane."

I touched the stones and tried to bring up a fond memory.

"So what's the plan?" D asked. "Or do we let Mark tell us what to do?"

"I like Lance's suggestion," Lilibeth said. "A couple of shifters might get past the spell. Do you know if Mark has asked Dolph for help?"

"I haven't heard anything," Lance said, "but then, I wouldn't be asked, right?"

"How often do the earth witches come into town?" I asked. There was a story about Lance and his alpha that was none of my business unless he chose to tell me. I was burning with curiosity, but we had a murder to solve.

"Some, never," D said. "A few of them are regulars. You met Violet, right? And Billy is always in with Mr. Macy, talking about herbs and things for spells."

"I was in their village the other day," I said. "At the chamber. I met Mr. Bark and Lily Valley. But that's all, and only two of the people I know are men."

"Are you worried about what Mark said?" Lance asked.

"That he'll throw us in jail if we keep investigating?"

"No, that he can't just go into the earth witch village and interview people."

"Does it mean we can't ask around?" I kind of pictured me wandering around the village talking to people until I noticed a missing earring, or someone said they knew who Mrs. Macy was meeting on the side.

"We can," D said. "Not officially of course, but if we can figure out who to talk to, we can just go ahead."

I guess the danger to me was higher, since I had no clue about what was safe here. I kept the thought to myself because I wasn't sure if they'd join Mark in trying to lock me away to keep me safe.

Dinner was eaten and a second beer sat in front of each of us. It was getting late, and I had plans that required me to be sober and awake tonight. "Why don't we try Lance's plan tomorrow? We need rest, and you all have work to do. We can give one more day to the investigation, and if we can't solve it, we let Mark do his job without us."

"It has been a long day," D said. "Let's head out and see each other for lunch?"

We all agreed and after downing the last of the beer, we cycled back to our homes.

44

I waited as long as I could before slipping out and getting the bike I'd put in the yard when we'd returned earlier. I worried that the bikes would be locked up for the night, and I couldn't ask because Lilibeth or D would have figured out my plan.

At least the spell bags didn't let off an alarm when I went out.

My phone was fully charged, because I would need the flashlight at some point on the road. The moon was up, so I had a dim view of the path, but I had no idea if it would be dark in the trees at my destination. The earth witch village was built under a lot of trees.

I hoped I'd find the final clue, but if everyone was tucked up in bed, I'd get my bearings and we'd all head in tomorrow.

The moonlight got me to the entrance to the village, but as expected, the trees blocked too much of it. And as soon as I put on my flashlight, I cringed. It was too bright. I covered it with my hands and blinked until the vivid pools of light in my eyes faded. I should have thought of bringing a scarf or something to minimize the blaze of white light.

I tucked it into the waistband of my jeans and pulled my tee shirt down, a temporary fix until I leaned my bike against the trunk of a tree. Then I had to keep it steady so the weight didn't pull the phone out of my jeans, or make it slide down to sit behind the zip. Being an unsanctioned detective was very complicated when you didn't really understand the world you lived in. Two weeks ago, there would have been enough light from the streets and houses, and I wouldn't have needed the flashlight.

It was quiet in the village, no big coven meeting or anything to get in the way of me sneaking around. There were spots of light from windows around me, and they illuminated the various pathways. Of course, there were no house numbers or names. I mean, I didn't have an address to go to, but it would have at least felt helpful. All it did was remind me I didn't plan very well.

I started walking to the first cottage. This one was more what I expected a witch to live in. Thatched roof, slightly crooked walls, and small windows. What I didn't expect was that the light showing me the way didn't come from candles or a fire; it was the flickery light from a TV screen.

The plan I'd just come up with was to find any of the earth witches I knew. That wasn't very many, and *knew* was an exaggeration. I'd met four. Billy Fern, Violet Bark, Alder Bark, and Lily Valley. I came up with reasons for the last three. I wanted to know more about the block on my power — was there a way to get past it? Billy, I didn't have a reason except to ask about herbs. We only shook hands in Mr. Macy's store.

I knocked on the door. The TV volume cut off, and I heard footsteps. The door opened and an old woman peered at me. "You're River's daughter," she said. "Come on in. I'll get us tea. You'll be wanting to hear some stories about when your mother lived here."

I stepped inside and followed her to a modern kitchen. "My mother was an earth witch?" I was completely shoved off my mission. No one so far wanted to talk about her, and this woman offered without being asked.

"Yes. Your father too. They both mixed more than I did, but earth witches are all different."

"Does that mean I'm one?"

She placed a mug of tea and a bowl of brown sugar in front of me. "Lemon and ginger," she said. "Good for balancing out your system."

I sipped. It was delicious.

"I don't think you are one of us," the woman said. "Oh, I'm Valerie Nightshade. I forget to introduce myself because I don't see many strangers. Your mother called you Cossi, so you have an earth name, but your powers seem to be more of the mind."

"I was in the chamber the other day," I said. "My parents blocked my powers. I was hoping to see one of the witches who did the ceremony. I want to go deeper than they did."

"Not yet," Valerie said. "Soon, but you have more important things to do. Your business is needed here, too."

"You know about that?" I finished my tea.

"There are very few secrets on Henbane, my dear. Yes. It will be easier for us to use your location than build more chambers. We've been using the tents on and off, but they need work, and we aren't prepared to do what it takes."

"Is it okay if I put that in my proposal?" I really needed allies to get it going.

"Of course, my dear. You should come back during the day, and we can go collecting signatures. Show we're behind you. Get that council in line." She laughed and patted my hand. "The Barks are the ones you need. They are four cottages over on this side of the path."

"Thanks. And I'll take you up on the offer of support. I should go now, so I don't keep Violet and Alder up too late."

"I'll be here for you, and we can talk about your parents any time you feel like it."

I put the mug in the sink and thanked her again.

Four cottages down wasn't like a street in Vancouver. The next cottage was just a faint light in the distance. I would need to be vigilant not to miss one.

"What are you doing here?" Mark stepped out of the shadows into my path.

45

When my heart stopped jumping out of my chest and I could breathe again, I smacked his arm. "What made you think that was a good idea?"

"You skulking around," he said grinning. "I guess I should give up on the idea that you might just one time listen to me. I'll settle for keeping you safe until our date."

"I'm here on personal reasons. I can keep myself safe. I don't know about the date yet."

"So if I said you could come with me while I talked to a few people about the murder, you'd say no thanks?"

"I can do my personal business tomorrow," I said before he could change his mind. "So, you're investigating?"

"Yes. Despite your expectations, I am doing everything I can to find out who killed Mrs. Macy. The tests didn't help. Someone is using a lot of energy to cover up the crime. I don't know if what you found today was a mistake on the killer's part or was planted to waste my time and throw suspicion on someone. But I have to follow up on the earth witch clues."

"What can I do to help?" I wouldn't get to tag along if I voiced my opinion of his lack of investigation. Clean slate and a lot of hope on my part that this would be over tonight.

"You came here to see some specific witches," he said. "Was it because you think one of them is the killer?"

"I only know four, oh, now five people who live here," I said. I gave him the names and how I knew them. Holding back information would drag out the case so, open book me. "I don't know if they are solid suspects. I was hoping to read their vibes."

"How do you trust your powers?" he asked. I was starting to wonder if I was still a suspect. "If there's a block, it could be covering up the full depth of what you can do."

"Wouldn't that have come up in the ceremony?"

"Maybe not. How long do you remember being able to read people?"

He was definitely after something specific. "As long as I can remember," I said.

"How old?" he asked. "I'm not being nosy. If your powers can't be trusted, then I'll try another tactic."

He was planning to use my ability to read people. I shouldn't feel so validated. He'd turned down any help I'd offered before. But, clean slate, Cossi. "I remember doing it in school. But my memories don't go back much before when I was nine or ten. Why?"

"I know when someone is lying. It makes me a better cop. But people lie about all kinds of things, not all of them related to a case. If you can read intentions, we're a good team. If you can't rely on it... I guess you'll still help."

So every time I didn't tell the whole truth, he knew? And didn't call me on it. He'd been trained to use his powers properly. Another spike of anger at my parents hit my gut. "The only times I haven't been sure about what I know is here. And someone told me people can shield against me. Like you do."

He had the grace to blush but didn't add anything to my statement. "We'll start with Lily and work our way back through the village."

LILY LIVED about a ten-minute walk farther into the forest. Mark had a flashlight and pointed out locations as we passed. There was a communal garden filled with wild grown plants — I mean, wild plants growing within a fence but not being cultivated. The Bark's residence was a house that would have fit in on a city street. Billy lived near a large circle of dirt enclosed in low shrubs.

"I don't think she's there," I said when we reached Lily's log cabin. "No lights. Maybe she's asleep."

"Wait here," he said. "She might be out back. I'll check."

He didn't wait for me to answer, and I was suddenly alone in the dark, standing at Lily's gate and fumbling for my phone to cast light.

I heard little sounds from the forest. Mostly just noises, scurrying or scratching. A fox barked but I couldn't make out words. Maybe I only understood when an animal was talking to me. That would explain why I wasn't inundated with chatter all the time.

My thoughts were stumbling all over themselves. It felt like Mark had been gone for an hour, and I hadn't checked the time before he left me. I held up my phone so it would come on. I wanted just the light from the screen. I let out a breath slowly to dampen my fear.

The jitters from the adrenalin had me jumping at every tiny disturbance. I couldn't walk it off because I would miss Mark when he came back.

I heard a step behind me. Someone grabbed my arm, then put his hand over my mouth.

"You should have stayed away," the words hissed in my ears. "Now you've made me do this."

The man rubbed an ointment on my wrist and whispered a few words I could barely hear, and then my eyes drooped closed.

46

I opened my eyes.

I could see the sky dotted with stars through a tiny window high on the wall in front of me. I was on a wooden chair in the center of the dirt floor. I could smell dried herbs around me, but not what they were because they were so mixed together. This was some kind of garden shed as far as I could tell. I stood and reached out my arms. I couldn't quite touch both walls, but it was close.

I hadn't been tied up, which was both reassuring and terrifying. I could find an escape route, but whoever grabbed me didn't care about me escaping. So either there was no way out, or I was about to be engulfed in flames.

I could test the first theory easily. My vision was able to pick out some of the room's features from the starlight and just getting used to the dark. Three walls were lined with shelves, all holding jars of dried petals, leaves, and twigs. The door must be in front of me, but I couldn't see a seam, let alone a handle.

Should I scream? Not yet. It would alert my captor that I

was awake, and I wanted that edge if he came back. And if I was in some remote spot on this island of remote spots, screaming would just give me a sore throat.

There was no convenient ladder to let me reach the window. It was too small for me to get through even if it opened, but I'd have a view of the surroundings. If there was any indication of other buildings nearby, I'd smash the glass and start screaming.

The only way up was the shelving. The window was above the blank wall that should have been a door. I tested my weight on the shelf to my right. Close to the wall, where it would be braced. It creaked but held. I scampered up so only the top shelf would have to hold me for any length of time.

My balance was scary. One foot on the shelf, the other swung out for balance. One hand on the wall in front of me, and the other hand grabbing the windowsill. I could see a path, and there was definitely a door. A glow of light in the distance grabbed my attention. It faded and popped back into sight. My imagination?

I couldn't smash the glass from my tenuous grip. The shelf creaked again, then shifted. A jar tipped over just as the brace gave way. I tried to turn the fall into a jump, but I landed on my butt.

Dust from the spilled herbs settled on my face, sparking a sneezing fit. If anyone was out there looking to rescue me, or come in and kill me, they would know I was awake.

Time to find the door. The man who put me here must have set a spell on the wall to conceal the exit. Maybe if I couldn't see it, I could feel it.

I stood, rubbed the ache in my backside and stepped to the blank wall. I visualized where the handle should be and reached out, closing my eyes before I touched the wood.

A big round doorknob.

I tried to turn it, but it didn't move. I used my other hand to feel for the lock. Not one you just turned to unlock. I needed a key and that wouldn't be inside with me. Even if I knew how to pick locks, there was nothing to use either.

I yanked on the door. This was an old building, maybe I could rattle the lock open. All I got was more dust in the air. I opened my eyes, hoping I'd broken the spell by touching the doorknob. No luck, my hand just disappeared into the darkness.

I picked up the chair and went back to the door. Now I knew it was there, I didn't need to see through the spell. The room was a bit tight to get a full swing of the chair, but I hit the doorknob with it and heard a crack.

I closed my eyes again and reached out. The knob came off in my hand, but the lock was undamaged. I turned sideways and started bashing the door. It moved a little with each contact but didn't conveniently collapse. I needed to find a weak spot before I dislocated my shoulder.

I ran my fingers across the surface to see what kind of door I was dealing with. It wasn't cold enough to be metal, so wood. It was like an old-fashioned barn door, thin planks held together by a frame and a diagonal cross brace. A kick at the bottom near the frame hurt my foot but did result in a crack in the slat.

I heard a shout from outside. My time was up. I put my back to the door and started donkey kicking to make a hole. If I could dislodge a couple of planks, I could squeeze out. I screamed as I kicked in case someone could hear and rescue me.

Two planks gave way at the bottom but didn't break. I got down on my knees and applied pressure. I wanted to open my eyes but couldn't risk losing sight of my target.

The nails gave out and let me push the wood aside. Now I opened my eyes and crawled outside, ignoring the pain as I scraped through the hole.

I was in the village.

Mark was chasing someone toward me. Billy Fern?

47

E verything went so fast after my escape.

Billy was the killer. He planned to keep me in the hut until he could sneak me off the island via the earth witch boat launch. He was going to block my memories and just drop me off to fend for myself.

Mark let Violet check me over. She gave me some salve to help the scratches heal and some witch hazel wipes for the bruising.

I could hear Mark talking to Billy as I let her check me over.

"Why did you kill her?" Mark asked.

"I didn't want to. I loved her," Billy said.

"Then why?" Mark asked again.

"She came," Billy said, nodding his head toward me. "We knew it was time to put everything to rest."

Mark looked over to me and then turned back to Billy. "We'll talk about this at the jail. You know what's going to happen."

Violet made me drink some tea before she let me go.

"The herbs will keep you alert for about an hour," she said. "It will get you home, and then you will sleep."

"I don't think I'll be able to sleep after this," I said.

"You misunderstand. I wasn't suggesting you should sleep. The herbs will take you there. Nothing sinister, don't worry. Tomorrow you'll remember everything. You should talk to Dr. Rene soon, but a good sleep tonight will help you on the first part of the journey to heal from this trauma."

IT WAS the best sleep I ever remembered having. No dreams that I could recall, and I woke up ready to take on the world. Phillip made me breakfast and gave me the morning off.

"Take a walk, or work on your proposal, do something that moves you towards the future. Brooding won't help you heal."

I had a task in mind. One that would bring me closure. Mark was going to tell me what the heck was going on in Billy's mind. He was the last person I would have picked as the killer; the last person I'd pick as Mrs. Macy's lover, too.

Mark was home and let me in. Roy licked my hand and told me he was proud of me. Why did his approval bring tears?

"I'd like to speak to Billy," I said. "He said it was something to do with me."

"Billy is gone," Mark said. "The council was waiting for us, and we pronounced his judgment."

My mouth dropped open. "No trial?"

"He killed a woman. He admitted it. He locked you up and planned to wipe your memories of the last three weeks and leave you to fend for yourself on the mainland."

All that was true, but maybe there were mitigating

circumstances. "Why did he say I was the reason he did it? Killed Mrs. Macy?"

"That wasn't important to his sentence," Mark said.

Roy gave me a little growl of warning.

"What sentence?"

"We lock his powers down and send him to a place where he can atone." Mark didn't want to tell me the details, but I didn't sense it was really a secret.

"Will everyone else know what happened to him?"

"The island will be informed that he was the killer," Mark said. "Officially, that is. By now, everyone will know the details."

"I meant his punishment. Is it secret from everyone or just me."

He sighed. "There's a place where all magical criminals are sent. It's like a monastery. Only for serious crimes. Billy is the first one we're sending, but other communities have darker experiences. His powers are locked down permanently. There may come a time when he can be trusted to come back, but he will never be able to cast spells."

I was silent. I didn't know how to process the information. Part of me was more than glad he was gone. The other part, the one still angry with my parents for blocking my powers, even temporarily, hurt for him.

48

"Someone told him to kill her because of you?" Lilibeth asked.

We were gathered at Jan's place for an early lunch. I'd updated them on every detail I knew.

"That's what I heard before Mark took him away," I said. "Did you know about this prison? Is it normal to act so fast after catching a criminal?"

D looked at Lance. He was asking if it was a good idea to tell me everything. Damn powers. It was hard to trust people when every little secret was written on their faces. Instead of trying to figure out my third power, I could learn to regulate my ability to read people. Not turn it off exactly, but mute it a bit when I wanted.

"Just tell me," I said. "How bad can it be?"

D grinned. "It's not bad. We're worried about inundating you with information. There's a lot to learn about our island. You should focus on what's important right now. Like your business."

"I can take it," I said. "Trust me, I'll let you know if I'm feeling overwhelmed." That was a lie, but he didn't have the magic to know.

"Yeah," D said. "I'm sure you will. You've been so open up to now."

I glared at him. He laughed and put up his hands. "Fine. We all know about the prison. It's a place for the communities to send criminals that can't stay where they live. Even if it's for a little time."

"There is more than one," Lance said. "Ours is for North America, there's one in South America. Europe has a couple. We don't know about all of them, but you can bet China has a couple, and India too. These places aren't crowded. Get the idea of the normals prisons out of your mind."

"So what kind of crimes get you sent away?" I asked. It was fine to say I shouldn't think of them like prisons on the mainland. Or on TV. But it was hard to banish the image of witches and other magical people dragging metal cups along bars in their cells. Calling out to the newbies with threats.

"It depends," Lilibeth said. "We haven't sent anyone before, and each community decides who needs to go."

"What do you mean, you've never sent anyone? I know you guys are probably way older than me, so like twenty years? A hundred?"

That set them all laughing until they were wheezing. I was getting pretty tired of not knowing when I'd been funny.

D was the first to get control enough to speak. "We're all around the age we look," he said. "As we get older, the difference between what we look like and our real age gets wider. Like, Jan is fifty, but you thought he was mid-thirties, right?"

"Okay. So Mrs. Vestum looks like she's a hundred and fifty years old," I said.

"She's two hundred and likely will make it to two-fifty," Lance said.

"That makes me feel even more sorry for Billy," I said. He'll be there for centuries if he got a life sentence."

"It's not horrible," Lilibeth said. "It's more like a spiritual retreat. Like a monastery. He'll be able to research anything he wants. He'll contribute what he uncovers to the rest of the witch world. Maybe at some point they'll invite him back to Henbane. Because he used a spell to hide his work and keep you locked up, he will never be trusted to actually do magic. But he's living in a nice cottage in an isolated part of the continent. He's looked after by the guards. Don't worry."

I had to let it go. It made no sense that I was sad for the guy who locked me in a shed after killing his lover. On top of that, he'd pointed the blame at me. "Fine, I guess I have loads of time now to concentrate on the Inner Spell."

WANT MORE?

Want more of Cossi? In A Spell In The Wrong Direction, she faces a kidnapping and a new killer in her search for a home. Use the QR code to join the investigation.

Please consider helping other readers to find Cossi and her friends.
Use the QR code below to leave a review and spread the word.

Want More?

FREE EBOOK

Claim your copy of Magic Will Out when you use the QR code to sign up for my newsletter and follow Cossi's search for her identity as a witch.

ALSO BY POPPY

For more books by Poppy Bridgeman

scan the QR code below.

ACKNOWLEDGMENTS

People think that the process of writing is solitary. That's not the case for me. I have help from so many people it would be hard to acknowledge everyone, but I'll give it a try.

The support and inspiration I get from my writer's groups is incalculable. The Vancouver Writers Social Group opens my mind to other ways of telling a story. The Royal City Literary Arts Society gives me the opportunity to meet and share with other writers who have more knowledge than I do. The Other 11 Months group is where I learn about getting the words on the page. And my critique group who helps me find the best parts of the story I want to tell. Thanks to all of the members of these great groups.

Last of all, but definitely a huge part of the process, my beta readers. These are the people who love stories and are willing, and more than able, to tell me if my finished story is ready for you, my readers.

ABOUT POPPY BRIDGEMAN

Hi, I'm Poppy Bridgeman, the cozy mystery alter ego of Canadian author P A Wilson. Poppy was "born" because sometimes stories need a gentler touch—with a little magic, a dash of humor, and plenty of sleuthing spirit.

As Poppy, I write the *Witch of Henbane Island* series (where witches and festivals collide with mysteries), the *EB Eats Culinary Mysteries* (a small-town diner, a determined heroine, and murder on the menu), and the *Pages & Paws Bookstore Mysteries* (a Devon bookshop, two mischievous corgis, and plenty of secrets tucked between the shelves).

When I'm not tangled in my characters' escapades, I'm happily tangled in yarn—I knit, weave, and doodle in sketchbooks between writing sessions. I also love to travel, finding inspiration for charming settings, quirky characters, and suspicious strangers wherever I go.

Home base is the Vancouver area, where I juggle writing as both Poppy and P A Wilson. Whichever name is on the cover, I'm always chasing the next story.